Already Gone

Jeremy Lawrence

ISBN: 1533317569
ISBN-13: 978-1533317568

DEDICATION

This book is dedicated to a friend who died way too young of cancer. Seeing him on his deathbed as he said goodbye to his loved ones, his only regrets the things he never got to do, made me realize life is short, you can't put off your life long dreams because it may suddenly be too late. I began pursuing my writing dream the day after his passing.

ACKNOWLEDGMENTS

I would like to thank every individual and business who made Independent Publishing possible. You have changed the publishing industry, forever. This book would never have seen print without you.
I would also like to thank my editors, Cate Hogan and Michael Garrett, my fabulous cover designer, Anna Dorfman, and all my beta and test readers. I couldn't have finished this novel without your advice, support, and encouragement.

Best consumed with *The Eagles Greatest Hits Volume I and II* playing in the background.

CHAPTER 1

Officer Carlie McBayne slammed the degenerate criminal into the glass doors of the police station. He turned his head just in time allowing his shoulder to take the impact instead of his face. The doors flew open startling everyone inside. He regained his balance and looked back at her—giving her as tough a look as a person can with their wrists handcuffed behind their back.

McBayne had a pretty face with dark brown hair pulled back and big, blue eyes. Thin, but solidly built, she could pass for the girl next door—if the girl next door was having a bad day and threatened to kick someone's ass.

Her perp, a meth head with bad skin and even worse teeth, had no idea what she really wanted to do to him. He was lucky there were witnesses around. He continued to plead his case but she ignored him—pushing him to the front desk protected by a wire cage. Sitting at a raised counter on the opposite side was the sergeant in charge.

She handcuffed her suspect to the bar in front of the cage. "Book him, Sarge." Fairly new to the police force, she still got a kick out of saying those words.

"What's the charge, McBayne?"

"Let's see." She thought for a second. "Drunk and disorderly, pandering, and public urination."

"Public urination? That's bullshit; that bitch just made that up," he said and looked around as if someone was going to come to his aid.

The officers in the immediate area looked up. "Ugh oh," the sergeant said and slid his chair back. Officer McBayne looked at him for a second, then reached into the sergeant's cage and grabbed a cup partly filled with coffee. She looked at it for a second like she was going to take a drink, then threw it into his lap.

The criminal jumped back but his handcuffs held him in place. A look of relief came over his face when he realized the coffee was cold.

"There, you even pissed all over yourself," she said.

He looked at the officer incredulously, then to the man behind the cage. "You saw that, right?"

The sarge laughed. "I didn't see anything. Looks like you pissed yourself just like the lady said."

Officer McBayne was a throwback to the old days before all the PC crap and cameras everywhere; when cops were treated with respect and criminals were treated, well, like criminals. It was just a matter of time before she got herself in trouble.

"If you aren't going to help me, I can't help you," she said to the perp.

"But I don't know anything."

"Then enjoy jail."

She signed the registration. Two officers came over, unlocked him, and took him away to the holding cell. "Give him a few hours, see if he volunteers any info. If not, let him go," she informed the sergeant.

"Okay, will do. You looking for anything in particular?"

"Nah, just trying to track down a couple dealers who are operating near the school. If he cooperates, he'll be back on the street by dinner time."

"All right... Hey, McBayne, the chief wants to talk to you."

"Oh shit, really? What about?"

She reviewed in her head why she might be in trouble. Seeing the chief was like getting called into the principal's office; rarely was it good news. The chief was a busy man and didn't have time for idle chit chat with first-year police officers. It was probably important.

"Don't know, could be a number of things. I doubt he's heard about the coffee incident yet," he said with a smirk.

She made her way over to two large doors and waved a plastic card in front of the black box on the wall, the doors opened. She headed down the hallway. On her left were several doors with translucent glass and names or titles printed on them. "Director of Diversity," "Public Engagement," the fourth office down said "Chief O'Halloran", he didn't need his position or purpose explained.

Officer McBayne could see the chief's outline through the window as he sat at his desk. She was half hoping he wouldn't be in. She knocked, opened the door a crack, and peeked in. "You wanted to see me, Chief?"

The senior police officer was a wiry, older fellow with thick glasses, thin arms and legs, and a pot belly. She had heard stories of the Chief's exploits in the past, he had some pretty big arrests back in the day. Since she's been at the station he seemed to spend most of his time doing PR, dealing with disgruntled employees, or performing administrative duties.

"McBayne, my favorite lady cop. Come on in, have a seat."

She sat down, trying to gauge the expression on his face—it didn't give away any clues.

"How's everything going?"

"Good, sir. No complaints."

"That's good to hear…no problems working with all men?"

"No, the other officers have been great."

"They have?" he said like he didn't believe it, then continued. "Well, I got a call from HQ." He paused.

She wasn't sure if she should know what the call was about. "Really?"

"Yes, your number's come up."

Oh crap—this is it, they've found out. About what she wasn't sure. "Umm, what number would that be, sir?"

"You made it—detective first class."

"I made detective?" She thought for a moment. "That was fast. I only applied to get some experience taking the test." *Maybe I shouldn't have said that out loud.*

"Well, they need women detectives. They're hard to find, harder to keep on the job. Have to keep up those quotas, or we'll have the harpies down our throat. Hell, if you were a Latino lesbian you'd be my boss by now."

"Well, I can speak a bit of Spanish, but I swore off the dyke thing a long time ago." She quickly realized who she was speaking to. *He's not one of your cop buddies, Carlie—cool it on the shock talk.*

"Really?" the chief said.

Too late.

"Yeah, turns out my mom was right. It was just a phase." She had a million questions, but one was the most pressing. "Listen, sir, do you think I'm ready for this?"

The chief, still distracted, didn't answer.

"Chief?" she repeated, "Do you think I'm ready to be a detective?"

He returned from wherever he was, nodded slowly, then answered. "Yeah, you'll be fine. You're raw, don't exactly go by the book, but you're effective."

"Thank you." She had no idea what he thought of her work, and that was the biggest compliment she'd heard the chief give anyone.

"I'm going to put you with Detective Waters. He's a straight edge, will keep you in line."

"Waters? I don't know him."

"He keeps to himself, doesn't socialize with the other guys; kind of an oddball I guess you'd say."

"Great," she said sarcastically.

"He might be gay, too, I'm not sure. We're not allowed to ask anymore, but they're sure as shit allowed to tell us. So, you two would have that in common."

"Like I said, that was just a phase. And it was only kissing."

CHAPTER 2

Detective Chance Waters was sound asleep, except for the twitching of his hand and the tormented look on his face. He was having the same dream that's haunted him for years, and was now starting to become more frequent. A man and a boy, trapped inside an overturned pickup truck, blood covering both of them. The seatbelts pinned them helplessly against their seats. The boy looked over at his father, trying to figure out what happened after he fell asleep. It was late at night as he rested under the warmth of a homemade quilt, the droning of the tires mesmerizing him until he couldn't keep his eyes open any longer. Then he was jolted awake.

He reached over and touched his Dad's shoulder, nothing. Touched his blood soaked cheek with the back of his hand, again nothing. The boy tried to speak, call out to him, wake him, but the words wouldn't come out. There was a commotion on the road outside of the shattered driver's side window. Through the blood dripping into his eyes he saw a pair of black boots approach, a metal object was placed to his Dad's head, then a loud crack and a flash of light.

Waters eyes popped open. He caught his breath and looked at the clock beside his bed, 4:47am. Once again, he didn't make it past five. He got out of bed and put on his jogging shorts, gray sweatshirt, and running shoes. He stopped in the kitchen to down a glass of orange juice, then headed out into the early morning Texas air for his morning run.

***

By 8am, Waters was sitting in the Chief's office, they're always the first to arrive for the day shift at the precinct.

"So, the Jennings case is closed, then?"

"Not yet, sir. I'm waiting on some results from the lab," Detective Waters answered in a respectful, slight Cajun accent. The chief stared at him. Waters knew what was next.

"Lab work? I thought the kid confessed?"

"I'm not a hundred percent. There were some odd things at the crime scene I want to confirm."

Chance Waters was a thin fellow in his early thirties, just under six feet tall. He had an innocent bordering on naïve look. He would be mistaken for a computer programmer long before a police detective.

"You're never going to be a hundred percent, Waters. We've talked about this before." The chief tilted his head and looked up at him. "Wrap it up by noon, got it?"

He nodded.

"By noon today," the chief repeated, stressing the word today.

"Yes, sir."

"Next item, your new partner."

"New partner?"

"You're getting a rookie named Carlie McBayne. She starts with you first thing Monday morning. I'm putting her in the empty cube beside you."

The detective fidgeted uncomfortably in his chair. "I don't believe that's necessary."

"Well, I believe it is. And you're going to have to train her; she's raw. She's been patrolling the streets, so she needs to clean up her approach or none of her arrests will stick."

Waters paused. "I think I'm more effective working alone."

"How about this, you start carrying your weapon and you can work alone."

The chief waited for a response. There was none.

"Didn't think so. You're getting a partner—can't have you getting shot on the job." A serious look came over the chief's face. "Now, we have to discuss something, your last two partners."

"Okay," Waters said curiously.

"You know they both requested transfers, right?"

He nodded.

"Do you know why?"

"Not really."

The chief reached to the corner of his desk and picked up a stack of papers. He shuffled through the pile and stopped at one containing a yellow highlighted section.

"Well, let's see here, blah, blah, blah, here we go." He raised his chin to see out of the bottom half of his bifocals and read from the paper. "'Chance Waters could bore a fly off a shit wagon'." He paused, then looked up at the detective. "Do you Louisiana boys know what a shit wagon is?"

"I believe it's a manure truck."

"That's right. Do you know how bored a fly would have to be to leave a manure truck?"

Waters lowered his head and spoke in a soft voice. "I can imagine."

"And your partner before that, let's see." He selected another paper from the stack and read the highlighted section. "'If I have to spend one more day with Detective Waters I'm going to put my pistol into my mouth and pull the trigger'."

The Chief looked up. "Waters, I can't have another suicide in this squad room. You know how much paper work that causes me?"

"I think he was being dramatic, sir."

"Really, that's what you think?" He paused. "I don't have time to play musical detectives, Waters. Make this one work, got it?"

The detective was out of protests and reluctantly nodded.

"Listen, I'm not saying you have to become best buddies, but you can't make it torture to spend eight hours a day in a car with you, okay?"

Waters returned a blank stare.

"She's your partner, she's on your team. We're trying to trick and confuse the bad guys, not each other." The chief's voice softened. "Now, you okay with a woman?"

"I guess so."

"Ever work with one before?"

"No, not really."

"She's a hot little thing. Is that going to be a problem?"

No reaction from Waters.

The chief let out a deep breath. "What I'm trying to say is, can you reassure me you won't be trying to fuck her?"

A visible blush spread over the detectives face. "No, that won't happen."

"Are you sure? You quiet ones worry me. You're the kind we

catch sniffing their car seat when they get out."

Waters looked puzzled. "I don't know what that means."

"The point is, you can't screw this up. I don't have the manpower. Don't bore her to death and don't try to fuck her. Got it?"

The detective nodded.

"I'm already losing two slots next year because we have to put in gender neutral bathrooms… Gender neutral bathroom." The chief repeated the phrase as if that was the first time he heard it. "What the fuck does that even mean? Does it have a urinal? What do they do for the little picture on the door, have a she-male with tits and a dick?" He looked at the detective for a response.

"Maybe a question mark?"

"Holy shit, Waters, that's perfect. You are a goddamn genius. I'm going to write that down." He wrote on his notebook while talking to himself, "Tranny Bathroom. Question Mark."

He looked up at the detective, more serious now. "Listen, Waters. You're a good detective, probably the smartest investigator I've ever known. I wish we had the time and resources to let you sit in a little office by yourself and crack all these unsolveds, but we just don't. I need you to get these day to day cases cleared faster, got it?"

"Yes, sir."

"I'm serious. Get these cases done quicker or I'm going to have to get someone else in here who can." He stared at the detective until he got a response.

Waters nodded.

"All right, now get out of here."

CHAPTER 3

"Ms. Daniels, we don't tolerate poor performance in this office. What do you have to say for yourself?"

The pretty, young, stylishly dressed woman hung her head. "I'm sorry, it won't happen again." She wore a tight black skirt, an almost see through white blouse, and high heels; corporate sexy, not corporate casual.

"I didn't hear you. Louder," her boss demanded. "And look me in the eyes when you speak."

She looked up. "Sorry, it won't happen again."

He held a paper in his hand and looked down at it. "These numbers are all wrong. Do you have any idea what you're doing?" He tossed the report onto his desk.

"I'll run them through again, sir."

The boss shook his head. "Did you even go to business school? Or did you spend all your time in college getting drunk and screwing frat boys?"

"What did you say?"

"You heard me. Were you screwing frat boys in college instead of studying?"

She paused. "Well, yes, I did screw one of them."

"I bet you did. I bet you loved it, too."

"He was on the basketball team. He was so sexy I couldn't help myself."

"That's disgusting. Ms. Daniels, come over here."

She walked around to the other side of the desk and stood in front of him.

"Now turn around." He put his hands on her waist and turned her so she was facing the door with her back to him. He leaned into her, pushing his groin against her backside leaving no doubt he had an erection. He placed his hands on the back of her blouse, then moved them down to her waist stopping at her hips.

"You like that, don't you Ms. Daniels?"

She shook her head.

He put his arm around her waist and pulled her tightly against him. "Can you feel how angry I am with you?"

She nodded.

His hand slid down the front of her blouse to the top of her skirt, then continued underneath it. He proceeded past her tucked in blouse to where her panties would start if she was wearing any. She gasped as his fingers made their way over her tightly trimmed mound, then between her legs. He could feel the warmth and dampness.

He leaned in and whispered into her ear, "No panties? You don't wear underwear to a professional office? And your pussy is soaking wet."

"Sorry, sir. It's almost laundry day and I'm out of clean clothes."

"Always with the excuses," he said and pulled her closer, his rigid penis pushing hard against her firm, tight cheeks.

"Would you have me wear something dirty?" she said in a brief moment of rebellion.

"What did you say to me?"

"All my underwear are dirty."

"That's it, bend over. You know the punishment for talking back to the boss."

She looked over her shoulder. "Please, sir, it won't happen again, I promise. I'm new. I don't know what I'm doing yet."

"Too late. You've already been warned once."

He grabbed her firmly by the shoulders and pushed her down, bending her over the desk. He pulled her skirt up over her shapely hips, exposing her perfectly round, toned ass.

"You're dirty, and now you have to be punished."

He unbuckled his belt, then his zipper, letting his pants fall to the floor. His penis was eagerly waiting to burst out of his boxers and discipline the scared young woman.

***

"Holy shit, Daniels, so that's why Victoria visits you at the office?"

Jacob Daniels grinned and shrugged. He was a handsome, all-American looking up and coming portfolio manager at one of the top firms in Dallas. He was having coffee with his boss, Ron Spiers.

Spiers quickly moved up the ranks of his company, sometimes utilizing questionable tactics, to become the CEO. The company was having record sales with him at the helm, so he had plenty of latitude to do as he liked. He was rugged, athletically built, and just starting to get some gray hair on the sides, but it made him look more distinguished.

"You know I can never look at Victoria the same after that, right?"

"It's probably best not to mention to her that I told you that story."

"You played basketball at Vanderbilt? Or was that just part of the fantasy?"

"I walked-on my freshman year; they needed players. I never played in a game. Victoria used to sit behind the bench and heckle me with her sorority sisters. Then she started flirting, too; that's how we met."

"Still, top of your class and played Division One basketball. That's pretty impressive. Maybe we should get the company team back together."

"I heard we used to have a good basketball team. What happened?"

"They blew it in the finals. I even brought in a tall black kid as an intern and they still lost. So, I disbanded the team and fired the coach."

"You fired him from coaching the team?"

"No, from the company. Losing is unacceptable, anywhere, anytime. You lose on the court you're going to lose in the boardroom, too."

Spiers took a sip of his coffee, still grinning—presumably from the story his protégé just told him.

Daniels returned to the business at hand. "So, how do you want to handle the Collins account?"

"How much is he investing?" Spiers asked.

"One point two mil."

"Nice. Split it sixty-forty. Forty percent in our funds where we get the big discounts, sixty percent in whatever he wants. Make him feel like he's part of the decision-making process."

Daniels nodded.

"If he doesn't specify, just spread it out over the standard high performing, low-risk funds. Can't go wrong there."

"Sounds good."

They took another sip of coffee and looked around at the clientele of the downtown coffee shop; returning interested looks they were getting from the attractive females. Both men oozed success and money.

"That story got me going. Might have to leave early today and surprise Mrs. Spiers."

Daniels smiled but didn't say anything.

"You know, Jacob, Emma and I mix things up a bit sometimes."

"I didn't know that," Daniels said fidgeting with the lid on his coffee cup.

"You'll see. After twenty years of marriage, you have to start spicing it up a little."

"You mean like getting a jet ski?"

"No, not exactly." Spiers paused. "Listen, we have another couple come over on Friday nights every once in a while. Have a few drinks, some gourmet appetizers, do some wine tasting. All attractive people. Could be good for your career for you and Victoria to stop by."

"Thanks, Ron, That sounds like fun. I'll talk to Victoria about it."

CHAPTER 4

Dr. Charles Browning pulled his Audi, which turned exactly two years old that week, into the service bay of the car dealership. Browning was a well-respected heart surgeon in Dallas.

"Hello, Dr. Browning," the attendant greeted him, "I'll get Mr. Williams for you." He picked up the phone and paged the general manager.

A voice on the intercom responded immediately. "Thank you, Steven. I'll be right down."

A few minutes passed and Williams arrived. Shaun was a light complected African American and the general manager of one of the busiest car dealerships in the State of Texas. He opened the passenger side door of Dr. Browning's car and got in. "Good afternoon, doctor. Ready for your new ride?"

"I sure am."

"Okay, pull up there." Williams pointed to a building ahead of them to the left. "Back of the body shop, by the car wash."

Dr. Browning drove forward. They passed several open car bays with grease-covered mechanics working on cars up on lifts.

"You don't want to try the coup? I'll let you demo it for a month if you want," Williams asked Browning, one of his many loyal customers.

"No thanks, maybe next time. I'm a sedan man; need my four doors."

"No problem. It's spotless; one hundred and fifty-three miles on it, brand new just like you like them."

"Perfect, love my new Audis."

As they approached the car wash bay, a young male employee pulled the new car out onto the driveway and stepped out. He took a rag from his back pocket and began to wipe off excess water left on the door jamb from the recent washing.

"Don't forget the trunk," Williams reminded him. "Hey, do you have your clubs in the back? I could maybe sneak out for nine."

The Dr. thought for a moment. "No, can't. Charlene's at home waiting for me with the interior decorator. She wants to remodel the living room. Like I'm going to have any say in it. Speaking of the better halves, how's Sky doing?"

"She's good," Williams answered as he opened Browning's trunk. "She's getting the charity bug again which always costs me money. I think she's just bored more than anything. She's working with Emma Spiers on something—clothing the homeless or shoeing the homeless, I forget. Do you know the Spiers? Her husband is Ron, some hot shot finance guy."

"Yeah," Browning replied. "I think I met him at a golf pro-am last year. He forked up the big money and played in Phil Michelson's foursome. Played pretty well as I recall, too, gave Michelson a run for a while. You know, I actually think he was pissed Michelson beat him."

"Well, we've been spending some time with them on weekends. They're a lot of fun, beautiful house, great taste in wine. Maybe we'll have you and Charlene tag along sometime."

"Sure, sounds good," Dr. Browning said.

The two men finished moving the Dr.'s things from the old Audi to the new one, said their good-byes, and Browning drove out of the dealership.

CHAPTER 5

Carlie McBayne made her way down cubicle row where the precincts detectives were located. It was just before 9:00 in the morning. Some people from the night shift were just finishing their work. She had a cardboard box containing some personal items.

She approached the cube that said "Detective McBayne" on a placard velcroed to the front wall. A smile appeared on her face, she had made it, hopefully, she was ready for this. The cube beside her said "Detective Waters." A slim man with brown, messy hair sat at his desk working on his laptop. His screen displayed some gruesome pictures of a dead body. If this wasn't a police station she would have thought the employee was screwing off on company time.

"Hello, Detective Waters?" she said.

He turned, looked up at her, then stood. "Yes, I'm Detective Waters."

She placed her cardboard box on the desk. "Carlie McBayne, nice to meet you." She reached out her hand.

Waters awkwardly took it. "Hello."

"So, we're partners."

"Yes."

A moment of uncomfortable silence. She broke it up by pointing to his computer. "Some light morning reading?"

"Oh, that's an article on blood patterns."

She looked at his desk. "Did you just move in here, too?"

"No, why?"

"Your work area is so clean. I mean, no pictures or knick knacks."

He cocked his head as if he didn't understand the concept. "I don't have any knick knacks. If I did, I would keep them at home."

"Oh." A few more moments of awkward silence. "Okay then, I

guess I'll get my stuff unpacked."

"Okay." He sat down and went back to what he was doing.

McBayne removed the items from the box; a coffee mug that said "World's Greatest Mom", the Mom was crossed out and it said "Aunt" underneath it, a stapler, sweater, and a picture frame with a white matte that contained a grid of smaller pictures. She placed the frame on the back of her desk, leaning it against the cube wall and making sure it was in a position so she could see it from her chair. She noticed Detective Waters watching her. "It's every Eagles album cover," she said excitedly.

"Who?"

"The band the Eagles; the best band in the world, ever, no?"

He shrugged and continued what he was doing.

The rest of the officers, detectives, and administrative staff were beginning to file in. There wasn't much commotion over a new person starting. She didn't know many of the detectives anyway.

She turned on her computer. A sheet of paper on the desk contained instructions on how to log in to the squad room's network, listed her ID and password, and contained a list of websites with videos she was required to watch.

All the training material was web-based now and pretty easy to follow. They mostly used Google and the internet for research. She started the series of videos. The stated purpose was to inform new detectives of standard procedures, security directives, and common laws. It soon became obvious they were really intended to protect the department from lawsuits, just a bunch of do this, don't do that, and other cover-your-ass precautions.

There was way too much material on criminal's rights—make that "suspect's" rights, and how to avoid infringing on them. She skipped through most of those parts.

She occasionally looked up to see what Waters and the other detectives were up to. *Please tell me they're not all working on the computer.* Detective Waters was still doing his research and taking notes. He answered a few phone calls, all of which sounded boring.

Almost two hours passed, finally she leaned over the cube wall and talked to her partner. "What do you do for lunch?"

"Oh, I bring mine." He pointed to a brown bag on his desk.

She waited for more information, looking him straight in the eyes. He finally broke.

"You can get something from the break room. Some people walk over to the cafe across the street."

"Oh, that sounds good. Do they have salads?"

"I don't know, I've never been over there."

"Well then, I'll let you know how it is." She grabbed her purse and headed out.

***

A half hour later McBayne returned from the café. Waters stood as she approached.

"We got a call. Are you ready to go out?"

"Oh, sure." She looked around her desk. "Yeah, I guess I'm ready."

She followed him down the hallway and outside the doors of the detectives' entrance to the station.

"Are we taking your car?" she asked.

"Yes."

Waters lead the way through the parking lot to his vehicle.

"Did they have salads?" he asked without looking at her.

"Yes, they did, and pretty good ones." She looked at him, not sure if he was really curious or just making conversation. "So, where are we going?"

"There's been a burglary at a laundromat down in Five Points. They usually send officers, but they're undermanned right now, so we'll take the call."

"Oh, okay. I know that area, that's my old beat."

"You worked Five Points?" He turned and shot her a surprised look.

"Yes, why?"

"That's not a very nice area. I'm surprised they let a woman patrol there."

Oh great, he's one of those. This is going to be fun. "Some of us gals can take care of ourselves, detective. Besides, it's all attitude. I learned that growing up in Chicago. You walk and talk with the right attitude, don't take any shit, the scumbags leave you alone. You can be scared to death, but it doesn't matter if they don't know it."

They got into Waters plain blue Ford sedan and headed down the road. More awkward silence followed. Finally, McBayne spoke. "So,

Chance, that's a peculiar name."

"It is?"

"First time I've heard it. What does it mean?"

"Nothing really. My mom and dad met at the Last Chance Saloon in Baton Rouge. They wanted to name me after that."

"I guess it's better than Last or Saloon." She smiled at him; nothing.

"*Chance*," she said to herself. "Chance, want to dance? Let's take a Chance." He didn't look impressed.

"Good thing you weren't fat when you were a kid. They would have called you 'Fat Chance'."

He gave her an annoyed look.

"Oh, I'm sorry. You weren't fat, were you?"

He turned his head to look at her. "No."

"Chance Waters; that would be a great porn name." She looked at him and said in a sexy voice, "Hey Chance, take off your pants."

He became visibly uncomfortable. She stopped.

The fifteen-minute drive seemed a lot longer, but they finally arrived at the laundromat. It was definitely in a bad section of Dallas. There was a broken window at the front, far end of the building, big enough to fit a person. As they walked toward the entrance, Detective Waters gave her the plan. "We'll take a report, get some pictures, check for witnesses, and see if there's anyone they know who might have done it."

They walked through the front doorway which was being held open by a wooden door stop. The owner, an old black man, met them by the front window. They obviously weren't patrons. Several people were doing their laundry as if nothing happened the night before.

"Hello, I'm Detective Waters. This is my partner, Detective McBayne."

"I'm Grady Johnson. This is my place."

"What happened, Mr. Johnson?"

"Um, let's see. I came in this morning around 6:00 and the window was broken. The cash boxes on several of the machines were pried open." He made a motion toward the broken machines. "It looks like they used a crowbar. I'm not sure how much money they got, maybe three hundred dollars."

Waters took out his phone and started taking pictures of the scene; the window, the machines that were broken, and the floor around them. Mr. Johnson and Detective McBayne watched him, patiently waiting for him to finish.

"I'm listening," he said and continued to take pictures.

"I imagine they used wire cutters to cut the lock on the pull-down cage."

"Do you know who might have done this?" Waters asked.

"Who might have done it?" Mr. Johnson gave him a puzzled look. "Any of the crack heads or gangbangers on this block. Listen, I just need to get a report filed so I can make an insurance claim and get the window fixed."

"Well, any information would help us find the culprit."

"Really? And what are you going to do when you find him?"

"Hopefully, get your money back and make him pay for damages," Waters answered.

"Detective, he's already smoked whatever he got from here."

They took notes and reviewed the crime scene. Waters inspected every foot of the building, including the alley behind it. Johnson gave them a list of names of local drug addicts and petty criminals. Most of them were first names only, nicknames, or just a brief description.

"I know some of these guys," McBayne commented as she reviewed the list.

They finished gathering information at the laundromat, returned to the car, and headed out.

They drove a couple blocks, when Detective McBayne spoke up. "So, that's it? We're going back?"

"Yes, and we'll file a report."

She thought for a second. "Can I try something?"

"Sure."

"Okay, take a left up here."

Waters took the next left. She had him make a few more turns then they came to a corner. A couple of black fellows were standing by the road watching cars coming and going, suspiciously leaning down and focusing on the drivers face.

"Pull over there." She pointed to a spot in front of the men.

As she rolled down her window, one of the men walked over to the car. "What do you need?"

The man immediately recognized her. "Oh shit, Officer McBayne?"

"Well, hi, Jamal, how are you?" she said in a mocking tone as if she was glad to see him. "I'm a detective now. Just stopped by to say goodbye. You won't be seeing me on the streets much anymore."

"Well, that's too bad," he replied sarcastically.

"Hey, I want to know who hit Johnson's laundromat last night."

"How the hell would I know?"

"Come on, someone knows. Ask around."

From the driver's seat, Detective Waters looked around nervously; keeping an eye on Jamal's partner.

Jamal thought for a second, then answered. "Sorry, can't help you."

"Where's Jitterbug? He would know."

"No idea about him either." He turned to walk away.

"Jamal, look at me." He stopped and turned back around. "You get word to Jitterbug, he needs to get in touch with me, or I'll find him and break my dildo off in his ass. Got it?"

Detective Waters had a surprised, if not horrified, look on his face.

The petty drug dealer nodded and returned to his corner.

"Jamal," she said.

He slowly turned and looked back at the detective. "I need to hear from someone soon, or I'll have to come back and close down the shop for a couple days, you hear me?"

Jamal nodded and returned to his post.

McBayne gave Detective Waters the drive ahead motion. "Come on, I'll buy you a cup of coffee. Let's see what happens."

***

A few minutes later the detectives were in the parking lot of a McDonald's having a cup of coffee.

Waters took a sip of his and made a face. "That's horrible."

"Don't like the gourmet coffee at the Mickey D's in the hood, Detective?"

He shook his head. *He wouldn't last long in these parts.*

"That was a colorful phrase you used back there. What does that mean?"

"Hmmm? ...Oh, Dildo?"

"Yes."

"You know what a dildo is, right?"

He blushed and didn't acknowledge.

"A fake rubber penis."

"Yes, I know."

And now he sounded insulted.

"I used to work with a tough cop, Perry Jackson. He taught me the ropes when I first started patrolling. Do you know him?"

Waters shook his head.

"He was always telling perps he was going to break his dick off in their ass." She laughed. "Anyway, I liked the visual, but I don't have a dick, so I can't use it. So, I started saying dildo instead."

"And what's the goal in using that phrase?"

"Intimidation. Let's them know you're serious. If you're willing to break your own dick in half to cause pain to someone, what else are you capable of?"

"Wouldn't that hurt him as much as the victim? I suspect bending an erect penis until it ruptured would be quite painful."

"Well, it's more of a saying than actually doing it."

"Is it effective?"

"I think so, and it's just fun to say. Try it. Pretend I'm the perp."

Waters shook his head declining her offer.

"Come on, say it." She leaned in toward him, pushed her finger into his chest, and said in a deep, angry male voice, "I'm going to break my dick off in your ass!"

Waters jumped, spilling his coffee a little.

"See?" she said, proving her theory.

They sat silently for a while, watching the down on their luck clientele of the McDonalds come and go. McBayne recognized a few of them, some she'd helped in the past, some she'd arrested, some she just roughed up a bit. Close to thirty minutes passed and McBayne's phone rang.

"Right on cue," she said and put the phone to her ear.

"McBayne, what do you got?" She listened for a few seconds, then hung up and turned to Waters. "Told you it worked. Let's go. There's an abandoned warehouse on 43rd and East."

She took a sip of her coffee as Waters backed out of the parking spot. "It's not that bad."

He looked at her, pulled over to a garbage can, rolled down his window and threw his cup into the trash bin.

They drove for a while, made some turns, and ended up in an even more desolate part of town. It was cold, gray, and windy; the area had a post-apocalyptic feel. Most of the buildings looked deserted and devoid of any signs of life. They pulled beside an old brick warehouse and scanned the area; nothing.

"Pull up there, at the end," she said and pointed to a spot a few hundred feet ahead of them.

Waters drove up then brought the car to a stop. As they got out of the car, McBayne turned to her partner. "Have your weapon ready just in case."

He paused, giving her the "I need to tell you something" look.

"What?"

"I don't carry one," he said.

"Don't carry one. Are you crazy?"

"I don't work this area much."

She shook her head in disbelief. "Okay. Let's go."

They walked to the side of the building. There was a stairwell at the far end with a metal railing and overflowing garbage cans beside the rail. She slowly moved toward it, looking around. Waters followed her.

She reached the opening of the stairs and pointed to the bottom. There was an old mattress with someone sleeping on it, covered by a dirty blanket.

"Stay here, keep an eye out," she told her partner. She took her gun from her side holster, took another look around, then started down the stairs.

An open doorway at the bottom of the stairwell lead to a dark room. It appeared to be empty. Detective McBayne approached the mattress. When she got close enough, she slowly reached down to grab the corner of the blanket.

Seemingly out of nowhere a pit bull appeared in the doorway of the room and started growling, startling her. "Shit." She jumped back against the cement wall of the stairs.

The dog, baring its teeth and taking on an even more menacing growl, stood in the doorway. Detective McBayne lifted her gun, prepared to shoot if it came any closer.

Waters witnessed the scene from the top of the stairs. He looked around frantically, then grabbed the lid off of one of the garbage cans and held it up in case the dog decided to come upstairs.

"Stay, stay. Good girl," McBayne said trying to relax the agitated canine. "I'm not a dog person. I will shoot you in the face. Okay girl." She looked down and noted the gender. "I mean boy." The dog appeared to be calmed by her voice. "Sit, sit."

Surprisingly, he did exactly as she commanded. He put his chin on his front paws and looked up at her like he was awaiting further instruction.

"Good boy," the detective extolled him.

The unconscious man wasn't affected by the disturbance, he probably just had his fix and was dead to the world. McBayne slowly grabbed the corner of the blanket and pulled it off the drug addict, keeping one eye on the dog.

Trying to inspect the entire scene without getting attacked by man or beast, she noticed a grimy pillow case beside the man. She reached down, tugged on it, and heard the distinct jingle of coins. *This feels like $300 worth of quarters.*

A crowbar was concealed underneath the bag. She grabbed it and heaved it underhand through the doorway. It made a loud clanging noise followed by an echo as it bounced across the concrete floor, finally coming to a stop.

The dog jumped up and turned toward the sound, then looked back at the detective. He was excited again, his stubby tail shaking back and forth.

"Go get it, boy; fetch," she told him.

The dog sprung forward and bolted after the metal bar, quickly disappearing into the fading light of the room.

McBayne looked up the stairs at her partner. They shared a surprised grin.

She grabbed the corner of the pillow case without disturbing the vagrant, turned, and hiked back up the stairs. Waters watched her closely, his tin garbage can lid at the ready in case the dog returned or the crack head awakened.

"Got it, let's get out of here." She looked down at his hands. "What's that?"

"Oh, nothing." He tossed the lid back onto the garbage can.

"Do you want to bring him in?" Waters asked, making a motion down the staircase.

"The dog?"

"No, the suspect."

"Suspect?" She looked at him oddly. "Why, he'll be dead in a month."

They returned to the car. Waters drove past the stairwell on the right and performed a wide U-turn in the next intersection. They headed back the way they came.

As they turned a corner and disappeared, the pit bull rose to the top of the stairs with the crowbar in his mouth. He watched them drive away with a disappointed look on his face.

They arrived back at the laundromat. Mr. Johnson had the glass cleaned up and a large piece of plywood installed over the shattered window.

McBayne and Waters brought the bag inside and returned it to the business owner. He opened the pillow case and looked inside. A surprised look came over his face. He smiled, thanked the detectives, and shook their hands.

The detectives returned to their car and headed back to the police station.

***

It was just past quitting time for the day shift as the detectives pulled into the police station parking lot. They got out of the car and headed back through the glass doors. There wasn't as much security at the detectives' entrance.

Walking down the hallway toward their cubicles, they saw Chief O'Halloran. He had a cup of coffee in hand and was attempting to drink from it without spilling as he walked. He stopped as the detectives approached. "McBayne, Waters, how'd the first day go? You check out that burglary?"

"Yes sir, we did," Waters informed him. "We found the culprit, retrieved the stolen money, and returned it to the owner."

"What?" the chief said. "That's it, case closed?"

Waters nodded.

"Chance Waters closed a case in one day?" He looked at his watch. "In four hours?"

"Well, actually, Chief, it was mostly Detective McBayne here who—

McBayne cut him off. "Sir, it was a pleasure working with Detective Waters today. I think I'm going to learn a lot from him."

The chief looked at her, back to Waters, then to McBayne again. "Well then, excellent. Keep up the good work, Detectives." He disappeared down the hallway and into his office.

McBayne started to walk toward her desk. She stopped, turned, and looked at Waters who was still standing in the hallway. She smiled at him. "See you tomorrow, Detective."

He watched her walk away.

CHAPTER 6

Several impeccably dressed women were seated at a decorated table in the back of a fancy ballroom. They had coffee, tea, danishes and other brunch items in front of them. A speaker at the podium was discussing the achievements over the past year of his charity in helping inner city kids get the proper training they needed to attend trade schools.

"Hi, I'm Emma Spiers," an attractive brunette said to the thinner, plainer looking woman beside her.

"Nice to meet you. I'm Jayne Thomas," she replied. They touched hands like fancy, elegant women do.

Emma wore a formal spring dress and filled it out quite nicely. Her cleavage was prominent and hard to ignore. If she had cosmetic work done, it was a fine job by the surgeon.

"Oh, who are you here with, Ms. Thomas?"

"Please, call me Jayne."

"Okay, Jayne dear. And you call me Emma."

"My husband Frank runs a publishing house in Ft. Worth. I'm here to bid on some charity items for him. He's supposed to be here." She made a motion toward the empty seat beside her. "But he got hung up. He usually does."

"Oh, how nice. My husband is Ron Spiers, Taylor Financial. He wouldn't be caught dead here."

"Fancy lunches not his thing?"

"Charity isn't his thing," Emma said and smiled, not appearing the least bit embarrassed. "What are you going to bid on?"

"I'm not sure. We don't need any gift items. Maybe the weekend in Cabo; Frank and I could use a vacation. He usually buys some items, then gives them to his employees."

"Oh, how sweet."

"Yes, that's my Frank."

The two ladies performed the greeting ritual with all the women around the table then continued their talk.

"That's a beautiful dress," Jayne said. "You have the most perfectly toned arms and shoulders, Emma. You obviously work out."

Emma folded her arms across her chest, feeling her muscles. "These are from swimming," she said proudly.

"Oh, that makes sense. Swimmers have beautiful bodies."

"Third place in the Texas state tournament my senior year," she said and smiled. "Sorry, it's my only athletic achievement. I have to brag about it."

"I would as well, Emma."

"I do cross fit now. It's pretty good, but I don't want to get muscle-bound like a lot of those women. Once my veins start sticking out that's it for me."

"Cross fit? You mean like climbing ropes and flipping over tires?"

"Yes, all that crazy stuff. Ron's trying to get me to play golf with him, too. Boring. And really, that's a workout, riding in a golf cart?"

"Oh, I know. Frank and I played with my father once. Never again."

A handsome, tall, dark-haired man approached the table from the doorway. He stopped behind Jayne and kissed her on the back of the neck. "Hello, dear. Sorry, I'm late."

"Hi, Frank."

He sat down at the empty seat beside her and nodded to the other women around the table. She slid a list of auction items in front of him, some were circled.

"Emma Spiers, this is Frank."

"Hello, nice to meet you. Oh my gosh, what a great looking couple you two are."

"Thank you," he said looking confused. "We try."

"You two are just adorable. Jayne said you're in publishing."

"Yes, I'm a managing partner at a firm in Ft. Worth."

"That's just perfect. I have a dear friend who's written the most beautiful children's book. Could you help us get that published?" She paused. "I'm sorry, that was forward. Maybe just some advice?"

"We don't handle that genre, but I can get you in touch with someone who can."

"That would be great. Thank you, Frank. You're as delightful as your beautiful wife."

"I must warn you, that's a tough category right now. It seems every celebrity on the planet writes a children's book these days, or has their people write it. And with the name recognition, they get first shot at getting published."

"I can just imagine. If Oprah said to bathe your kid in BBQ sauce, half the mothers in the country would take her advice."

Frank reached into his suit pocket and handed her a business card. "Here, give me a call. I'll have my secretary set something up."

The group continued the chit chat. Frank bid on a few items. Eventually, Emma got up and grabbed her purse. "Well, I must be going."

"You're not bidding on anything?" Jayne asked.

"No, not today."

Frank stood, shook hands, and prepared to say goodbye.

"So, what do you two do for fun?" Emma asked eagerly.

Frank and Jayne looked at each other. "Nothing outrageous," Jayne replied. "We love good food, dancing, fun company."

"Oh perfect. We've had the most delightful group of people meet at our house the last few weekends. If you're not busy you should stop by."

"Sure, that sounds like fun," Frank answered.

"Great. I'll be calling you Frank. That wasn't a courtesy offer about the book was it?"

"I gave you my card, that means business."

Emma shook hands with Frank, kissed Jayne on the cheek, and left the ballroom.

As she left, Frank gave Jayne the "what was that all about" look. She shrugged.

CHAPTER 7

The door to Ron Spiers office opened and his secretary poked her head in. "Mr. Spiers, it's Howard Andrews from accounting to see you. Do you have time?"

Ron looked at his watch. "Yes, send him in, but tell him I only have a few minutes."

She nodded and left.

Howard Andrews entered. He was better dressed and more stylish than your typical corporate accountant. He looked at the floor to ceiling windows behind Spiers' desk.

"Hell of a view, Mr. Spiers."

Ron nodded.

Howard looked at the table and wall to his right. They had photos and memorabilia displayed of Ron with different sports stars and Texas celebrities including a signed basketball from Mavericks owner Mark Cuban, and a football from Cowboys legendary Coach Tom Landry.

The two men shook hands. "Hello, Howard. Are you getting settled in okay?"

"Yes, I am. Everyone's been very nice."

"Good. You let me know if they're not."

"Thank you, I will."

"Did you find an apartment?"

"Yes. Nice place just west of the city. My furniture should be arriving next week and I can move right in."

"Fantastic. I forget, did you say your wife is coming out with you?"

"Um, no, she's not. She's going to stay in Tallahassee."

Spiers gave him a puzzled look.

"We're working some things out."

"Oh, got it."

"I'll get right to the point, Mr. Spiers, I know you're busy. I'm having trouble getting access to our electronic records. No one seems to know where they're stored."

"Really? That's odd. Did the ops team get an account set up for you?"

"Yes, and I can see all of the company accounts, except yours."

Spiers rubbed his chin with his thumb and index finger. "You know we've had trouble with continuity in our accounting department?"

"Yes, I've heard. Four managers in the last five years."

"And that's part of the reason for the turnover. Those records should have been digitized long ago. Sometimes it takes a while to spot incompetence. Hopefully, you'll outlast your predecessors," Spiers said and smiled at Andrews.

"Well, let's hope so."

"I know our last accountant was working on a project to move them from paper to electronic, but he left abruptly and I never got an update from him."

"That's odd. No firms are paper based anymore. It's more work and more expensive to stay on those archaic systems. Paper statements have to be manually prepared every quarter."

"Well, Howard, that's why you're here."

"Do you know the last time we were audited? Most auditors won't even accept documents in paper form."

"No, I'm not sure of the exact date. Two years ago maybe."

"I've been reviewing some of your top investors. Their yearly average return is pretty high, that's usually a red flag," Andrews informed his boss.

"What do you mean?"

"I've only reviewed a few of the accounts because I have to do it by hand, but the yield is several points above market average. The Feds typically require a review of them if that's the case. You know with what's been going on the last few years."

Spiers looked confused.

"Ponzi schemes. They're highly sensitive to that since the Madoff scandal. If I can't trace the investors' money to their transactions and justify the return, they start looking into it."

"Okay then, I'll see if I can find out where the electronic records are stored. For now, let's just keep this between us. Okay, Howard?"

Howard nodded and left Spiers' office.

CHAPTER 8

Detective waters took a quick look at his partner in the passenger seat of his car. Her big blue eyes were focused down at her phone checking messages. Things were going better than he expected—at least he hoped. She wasn't impatient and rude to him like his previous partners had been.

"Have you ever been to the forensics lab?" he asked her.

She looked up. "No, I haven't."

They didn't have any case work going on at the lab, it was just a slow day and a good time to introduce Detective McBayne to the lab guys and learn the process.

"Really, not even as a cop?"

"No, everything I did was on the street. No need to get fingerprints. If it was a high visibility crime we had the mobile lab come out."

"It's about forty minutes away, depending on traffic. It's not much; cutbacks have decimated the facility. It used to be decent, but they can't afford any new equipment or software. They're way behind in technology now."

"Oh, good thing we're checking it out then."

That's probably sarcasm.

"Well, they can help with the basics." He thought for a second of what that could be. "Fingerprinting I guess."

He pulled out of the station parking lot, made a few turns and headed north past University Park toward the outer belt.

"They used to have a few more labs, too, but they consolidated most of them into one. Now the backload is even worse and it's farther away."

McBayne gave him a half-interested smile. "Mind if I turn on the radio?"

"That's fine."

She pressed the power button and quickly went through the stations before he could even tell what song was playing.

"What are you looking for?" he asked.

"The Eagles."

"You're looking for one band?"

"Yep."

"You should get satellite radio. I bet they have a station that's all Eagles songs."

"I'd love to have that. As soon as I get a raise."

"Satellites will be old technology by the time that happens."

She laughed in cynical agreement.

"The Eagles; that's the picture you have in your cube?" Waters asked.

"Sure is. I love the Eagles. I'd jump everyone in that band."

"Aren't they like seventy years old?"

"Not now, twenty years ago. Maybe thirty."

She cycled through the stations again; nothing. "And I'm going to make it to Winslow, Arizona before I die."

He looked at her. "Why Winslow, Arizona?"

"Because, I'm the girl in the flatbed Ford…from the song."

"What song?"

"What song? Are you kidding? 'Take It Easy'."

"Take it easy with what?" He quickly tried to figure out what he said wrong.

"No, the song, 'Take It Easy', by the Eagles." She put her fist to her mouth like a microphone and started singing the key verse of the song referring to the town in Arizona and the girl in the flatbed truck.

"Oh, right, I've heard that one."

"Did you know that Jackson Browne originally wrote the song, but couldn't finish it, so Glenn Frey took it over and added that verse?"

"I don't know who either of those people are," Detective Waters informed her.

"Never mind," she said and looked out the window. "I once rebuilt a Ford truck and turned it into a flatbed." She looked over at her partner. "Then I quit school in Chicago and headed down to Arizona."

"What happened?"

"Truck broke down in Tennessee, couldn't afford to have it fixed. So, I got stuck bartending there for a couple years. Someday, though, I'm going to finish that trip."

She had an odd look on her face, a combination of sadness and regret. It was the first time he'd seen her be anything but decisive and bold in the short time they'd been working together. He decided to change the subject. "How'd you end up in Texas?"

"Same old story. Followed a boyfriend down here."

"Really?"

"What do you mean, 'really'?"

"I don't know, I can't see you following a guy I guess."

"Yeah, it was a big mistake. Won't do that again…Where are you from, Detective? I can detect an accent, but not sure what it is."

"Northern Louisiana, outside of Shreveport."

"Oh, that makes sense," she said and nodded. "I thought I heard a little Cajun."

They drove for a while, some song that sounded like all the other new songs was playing. Frustrated, McBayne turned off the radio.

"What kind of music do you like?" she asked her partner.

"I'm not a big music guy."

"Really?" she said sarcastically.

He smiled. "I like country songs, I guess, about the rodeo."

"As opposed to hip hop songs about the rodeo?" She laughed, amused by her own joke. "Rodeo songs. Are you kidding? They're all so sad."

"Not all of them."

"Really? Name one where the cowboy doesn't pick those stupid steers over his woman. If you can find me a happy rodeo song I'll show you my tits"

He glanced at her, blushing at the dirty talk, but couldn't think of a happy rodeo song.

"If you lose your man to a goddamn steer you're doing something wrong."

CHAPTER 9

Five sexy, well-dressed women, some of Dallas' finest, sat in a semi-circle around a cocktail table with fancy drinks in front of them. Long legs, high skirts, and revealing blouses were the style for the evening.

Emma Spiers, the wife of Ron the high finance guru, was looking elegant as usual in a classy top highlighting her hourglass figure. Beside her, Victoria Daniels, wife of Jacob—Ron Spiers protégé—was showing off her long legs and slender figure. Next was Sky Williams, the strawberry blonde spouse of Shaun the Audi dealership's GM. Beside Sky was book publisher Frank Thomas' wife Jayne. And finally, the youngest and sexiest of them all, Charlene, the recent bride of Dr. Charles Browning, the hottest heart surgeon in Texas.

The club played house music and the dance floor was filled with other well-dressed, beautiful, successful people. The music wasn't so loud that it drowned out conversation. The ladies appeared to be genuinely interested in each other's conversation, they weren't looking around trying to spot better options like a lot of the other patrons were.

Emma Spiers raised her glass for a toast. "Cheers, ladies, I think we still got it."

They gently clanged glasses and took a sip of their martinis, expensive wine's, and brightly colored vodka drinks.

"We're not talking about you, Char, that was self-assurance for us older gals," Victoria Daniels said.

Charlene smiled and tipped her glass toward Victoria. Although several years younger than the rest and from a different background, she was fitting in well.

"How's the charity business going?" Jayne asked looking at Emma and Sky.

"Good. We raised over forty thousand for disenfranchised youth last week," Sky answered.

"What does disenfranchised mean?" Charlene asked.

Emma and Sky looked at each other. Emma answered. "It basically means your parents suck. They didn't want you, dad's not around, mom is more interested in getting high and partying."

Sky gave her a disapproving look. "That's not always the case. A lot of times it's environmental or societal reasons for the breakup of the family unit."

"Sure it is," Emma said dismissively and took a sip of her wine.

"Let's not judge others unless we've walked in their shoes," Sky said to Emma.

"I've been in those shoes. It's all self-inflicted misery. You can get out of it if you want."

"How can you do so much work for those charities if that's how you feel, Emma?" Jayne asked.

"I do it for the kids. It's not their fault they lost in the parent lottery."

"Enough of the depressing talk, ladies," Victoria broke in. "What do we think about that outfit." She made a motion toward a group of three women at a table several feet away. The one they were talking about had a blouse with a ridiculously high collar, almost turtleneck high, and bell bottom dress pants.

"Hmmm, trying too hard I think," Jayne said.

"Some outfits just look better at home," Charlene added.

"And should remain there," Victoria said.

Two young men were sitting at the table behind the one the women were focused on, they raised their glasses and nodded to the ladies. They apparently thought the women were looking at them.

Emma returned a forced smile. "Now you've done it," she said looking at Victoria, "they think it's their lucky night."

"Poor bastards," Jayne added.

The girls continued their conversation; updating each other on the week's events, what their husbands were up to, and the latest stories of crazy family members and mother-in-law's. Some were updates of ongoing dramas.

The waitress came to the table. "Ladies, those two men would like to buy you a round of drinks." She made a motion toward the two who thought the ladies were looking at them.

"No, they're not buying us a drink," Emma informed the waitress. "Put their next round on our tab and tell them to stop gawking and come over here."

The waitress smiled. "And another round for everyone else?"

All the women nodded except Victoria, she was distracted, checking out the occupants of a table in the back.

"Vicki," Charlene said, "do you want another wine?"

"Yes," she answered, then looked at Charlene, "and it's Victoria."

"What?"

"She doesn't like to be called Vicki," Emma informed Charlene.

"Oh, what's wrong with Vicki?"

"Vicki is a girl who gives free hand jobs in the parking lot of a bowling alley. Victoria is a smart, sexy woman who men are intimidated to talk to because she's so classy."

"Okay," Charlene answered, still looking confused.

"Remind me not to name my daughter Vicki," Jayne said.

"Oh my God, are you pregnant?" Sky asked her.

She downed what was left of her vodka and cranberry, looked at the girls, and said, "Nope." Then she said to the waitress, "Make mine a double."

The waitress left to get the drinks. A few minutes later she returned to the table of the young men and delivered their complimentary drinks. She made a motion toward the women's table, obviously telling the men who paid for the drinks and conveying the invitation. The men looked at the waitress, then got up and made their way to the ladies table.

The taller, dark haired one, obviously the more confident of the two, tipped his glass and spoke. "Thank you, ladies, that was very nice."

The women nodded.

"Grab a chair and join us," Emma said.

The two men placed their drinks on the table and grabbed two chairs from a nearby empty table. The dark haired one put his chair beside Emma, his friend beside Charlene Browning.

"I'm Steve, this is Jason," he said. Steve's hair, clothes, and facial features were like that of a daytime TV leading man, almost too perfect. Jason looked like he wasn't trying as hard, in fact, he seemed like he didn't really want to be there.

"Nice to meet you. I'm Emma. This is Victoria, Sky, Jayne, and

Charlene," Emma pointed to each of the ladies as she listed their names.

Steve watched Emma's introductions carefully, his lips moved as he repeated the women's names under his breath.

"Okay, boys, we're not desperate cougars looking to bang young studs to make us feel good about ourselves," Emma informed them. "You won't be getting laid tonight, at least not by one of us."

Steve and Jason almost spit out their drinks. The other ladies smiled and waited to hear what Emma was going to say next.

"Come on, Emma, give them some credit, that took guts to come to our table," Jayne said.

"That was impressive," Emma said, followed by an approving nod.

"I'm just curious, which one of us were you planning on hitting up?" Victoria asked.

Jason, the shy brown haired one, made a motion to Charlene, then immediately looked down and blushed.

"Of course," Victoria said, "they all love Char."

"And you?" Emma said motioning toward Steve.

He thought for a moment. "Any of you, you're all hot."

The ladies all laughed.

"That's the right answer," Sky said.

"All right boys, let's have a look," Emma said. "You're handsome. Fairly tall. Nice hair. You're young, dress okay, don't act like meatheads."

They smiled and nodded having passed the test so far.

"I'm going to give you a tip. You have to have money, style, and be good in bed to land hot, classy ladies."

"I have all that," Steve answered.

"You're good in bed, too?" Victoria asked.

"Yes, he is," Jason cut in.

Everyone looked at him.

"How the hell do you know?" Emma asked.

The ladies laughed. Steve shook his head like he'd just lost a large pot in poker. Jason became red with embarrassment.

"That's what his old girlfriend told me," Jason replied.

"Good save," Victoria said.

"Listen, that bi-sexual crap isn't attractive, don't go there. Real women want a real man, got it? Especially in Texas," Emma informed him.

"No, we're straight, seriously. I don't know why he said that," Steve said.

"Okay. And that metrosexual crap works in New York and San Francisco, but not here," Emma added. She waved to the waitress who quickly came over to the table. "We'll have a round of shots, lemon drops. What do you fellas want?"

"We'll have the same," Steve answered.

"No, you won't," Emma cut him off. "Don't do girly drinks. Order a whiskey, straight up."

Steve paused, then looked at the waitress. "We'll have two whiskeys, straight up."

The waitress left to get the drinks.

"What does straight up mean?" Jason asked.

"That's cute," Charlene said smiling at Jason.

"It means they chill it with ice. But don't get it over ice, that's not manly either," Emma said.

They continued their re-training of the two men a bit longer. Emma let the pretty boy know he was trying too hard, everything was too perfect, then she messed up his hair. The waitress returned with the shots. They did another group toast, then downed the drinks.

"So, what other girls in this place are you interested in?" Emma asked the young men.

"You ladies were it," Steve said motioning toward their table.

"I kind of like her," Jason said pointing to a cute but plain looking waitress working another table.

"Now that's smart. Good choice," Emma said to Jason. She shifted her focus back to Steve. "You need to be more realistic. Stick with the girls you have a shot at. No one at this table."

Steve nodded.

"Look at these girls," Emma said motioning toward her friends. "See the rings, the necklaces, the expensive shoes. They're not looking for a man. That's the look of satisfied women."

Steve nodded.

The plain looking waitress walked by their table. Emma reached out and gently took her by the arm. "Hi, sweetheart, what's your name?"

Surprised, she answered like it was a quiz hoping she got the answer right. "Terry."

"Terry, do you see that young man," she said pointing to Jason. "Do you think he's cute?"

She blushed, "I guess so."

"Do you have a boyfriend, dear?"

She shook her head.

"Do you have plans tomorrow night?"

Another head shake.

Emma opened her purse and took out a hundred dollar bill. She reached across the table and handed it to Jason.

"That's a hundred dollars, Jason is going take you somewhere nice for dinner tomorrow, is that okay?"

Terry nodded.

"You're not an ax murderer are you?" Emma asked Jason.

He shook his head.

"Steve, is he an ax murderer?"

"No."

"He's a gentleman? He'll treat Terry like a lady?" Emma asked Steve.

"Yes. Great guy. I'd let him date my sister… if I had one."

Emma looked at Terry. "Great, then give him your phone number."

Still appearing completely befuddled, Terry wrote her number on the top page of her menu pad, tore it off, and handed it to Jason.

Jason, almost as confused, looked at the number then up at Terry. "Okay then. I guess I'll call you tomorrow."

The waitress nodded and walked away, but not before looking back one more time seeming to confirm what just happened.

"Okay, boys, we have to get back to our girl talk. It was nice meeting you." Emma gave them the shoo motion with her hand.

The two men looked disappointed. They stood, put their chairs back, and started to leave.

"Thanks for the drinks," Steve said.

"And for getting me a date," Jason added, his face lighting up.

"It was nice meeting you," Sky said as they turned to leave.

"Have fun on your date," Charlene said to Jason.

He smiled and nodded.

"That was fun," Emma said. "Now, ladies, it's time to play truth or truth, ready?"

They nodded in unison.

"Okay, let's say your husband is driving the rest of us girls around in his car. And God forbid, it spins out of control and goes over a cliff. All of us are killed, including your husband."

"Emma," Sky said in surprise.

"Just pretending. Now, you have your choice of being consoled," she made the air quotes as she said 'consoled', "by one of our husbands." She smiled a wicked smile. "Which one would it be, and why?"

The girls all grinned and went into deep thought.

"Why, Charles of course," Victoria said and looked at Dr. Charles' wife, Charlene. "Sorry, dear, I would need a big swimming pool to make me feel better."

The ladies laughed.

Sky spoke up next. "I'd talk to Frank," she said looking at Jayne Thomas. "He's just so sweet, I bet he'd be great after something like that."

Jayne nodded in agreement. "Yes, he would."

"Ron." Charlene said and looked at Emma. "He just seems like he would take charge and make everything better."

Emma smiled. "He'd take charge, not sure how much better he'd make things, though."

The girls looked at Jayne Thomas.

"I can't decide, I guess I'd take them all."

"Gross! At the same time?" Victoria asked.

"No, not like that. To console me, right?" She paused. "What about you, Emma?"

Emma thought for a moment, then looked at Sky Williams. "Shaun. I think his strong arms around me and that muscular body would make me feel better. Sorry, dear."

"I understand, they do help sometimes," Sky confirmed.

Emma flagged down the waitress and ordered another round of shots.

CHAPTER 10

Frank Thomas sat in his king-sized bed, covered from the waist down by a satin sheet. He had a laptop balanced on his legs and was finishing some work. The large flat screen TV on the wall across from the bed was showing an On Demand adult movie with no sound. Two women were engaged in the sixty-nine position. Another laptop at the foot of the bed played an Internet porn video. Two guys were double teaming a rough looking blonde.

"You ready?" A woman's voice asked from the bathroom.

"Yes," he replied.

His wife, Jayne Thomas, opened the bathroom door. They met at a publishing company and have been married a few years now. She was a Jr. Editor and he was climbing the executive ladder, very quickly.

She approached the bed seductively, wearing a sexy white nightgown, white satin stockings that hooked into her garter belt, and white high heels.

"You ready for this?" she said in a sexy voice, then looked down at what he was doing. "Frank, are you working?"

"Almost done. Just have to send this email," he said without looking up. He typed some more while she stood there and watched. Finally, he hit the send button.

He switched the computer screen to another porn video that was playing in the background, leaned up, and placed it at the end of the bed across from the other laptop. "Okay, let's do this."

Jayne sauntered to the end of the bed and stood between the two computers. She stared at him with sexy bedroom eyes, put her arms over her head, and started to move her hips, dancing like a stripper— well, a stripper on her first night of work.

"Like what you see?"

"Oh, yeah, I like that," he said, but couldn't help but laugh.

"Frank, come on!"

"I'm sorry, it won't happen again, continue."

She turned around, spread her legs and bent over.

Frank smiled. "Okay, that's better.

The thin white panties barely covered her lady parts. She looked back at him between her legs and shook her ass.

"Yeah, that's good." He reached under the covers and grabbed himself.

She stood up, turned, and leaned forward onto the bed, sliding her panties down her legs until they got stuck on her high heel, she struggled to free them. Finally, they released and she flung them at Frank like a sling shot. He bit the air as they flew by like he was trying to catch them with his teeth.

Like a cat, she crawled slowly toward him between the two computers. Her high heels fell off her feet onto the floor. She glanced up at the neon clock display on the nightstand, seven twenty-seven in the evening.

Her breasts rubbed against his feet and legs under the silky sheet as she continued toward him, stopping when her face was over his groin. She straddled his leg, rubbing herself against him, and lowered her mouth to the bulge created by his penis under the sheet. She rubbed her lips and chin against him, then playfully bit down lightly on his shaft.

"Frank, come on. How can you not be hard yet?" She pulled down the sheet and looked at his semi-erect penis.

He shrugged. "I don't know. These pornos aren't really doing anything for me.

"Well, is this doing anything for you?" she said and gestured toward her mostly nude body. "Hand me that," she said and pointed to a tube of KY Jelly on the nightstand.

He grabbed it and handed it to her. She unscrewed the top, squeezed some onto her hand, and tossed the tube back onto the nightstand. It landed on a Cosmo magazine, right on the headline that said, "How to please your man," and bounced off onto the floor.

She grabbed Frank's penis with her lubed up hand and started stroking it, concentrating on the sensitive areas all the love making books talk about. She went faster then slower, alternating pressure like the magazines say. Finally, he started to get hard.

"That's better," she said and lowered her head. She put her mouth down there, teasing with her tongue and looked up at him. Finally, he was ready. He tilted his head back and closed his eyes.

She stroked him for a few more minutes, massaging his testicles, then crawled on top of him. Straddling his waist, she slid her pussy against this penis—slowly at first, then faster. She was getting wet and started to moan. She continued that for a while then looked down at him.

Jayne pulled her bra down exposing her smallish, but perfectly shaped breasts. She thrust them forward into his face and continued to grind on him, not letting him penetrate her. She was getting wetter and more excited.

"Pinch my nipples."

He reached up with both hands and did as he was told, squeezing her nipples tightly between his index fingers and thumb. "Yes, like that," she said and moaned, a quiver shooting through her body. "Fuck, that feels good." She leaned in and kissed him passionately, pressing every sensitive part of her body against him.

She stopped and spun around on his chest, facing backward—getting a great view of all the porn videos, but her attention was on what her husband was doing. She leaned forward toward his feet, reached between her legs, and guided his penis into her. "You like your backward cowgirl, don't you?"

He nodded.

She continued to gyrate on him, bending his penis backward and forward, rubbing it hard against her clit. She did that for a while then turned back around to face him. His manhood easily found her wet opening and slid back in. She started to ride him, harder and faster, grinding her teeth and pressing herself against him.

Finally, she couldn't take it anymore. She moaned deeply, said, "Oh, yes," and pulled herself closer to him, quivering. Her body shook and her limbs collapsed around him.

It took several seconds to recover. She turned her head and looked at the clock, it said seven thirty-nine. "Nice, twelve minutes. Did you come?" she asked.

He shook his head no.

"Good boy. " She rolled off of him and went back into the bathroom.

CHAPTER 11

Detective McBayne watched her partner's face light up as the roller skating waiter returned to the car with their meals. He pulled up to the window and stopped, holding the tray filled with food in perfect balance.

Waters smiled and looked at his partner like they just saw an awesome magic trick. The young waiter-entertainer handed him the tray with two burgers, two fries, a Coke, and a chocolate milkshake through the open car window. Waters gave him a twenty and a five dollar bill.

"Extra thick shake, right?" he confirmed.

"Yes, sir. I'll be right back with your change."

"That's okay, keep it."

"Thank you. Enjoy your meal," he said, and with a couple quick leg kicks, he was gone, weaving through the other cars as he crossed the driveway separating the detective's car and the restaurant.

"Really Waters, a chocolate milkshake? What are you ten years old?"

Waters took off the lid and raised the shake into the air, tilting the opening toward his mouth. He tapped the bottom with his other hand so the thick ice cream dripped slowly into his mouth

"Do you come here for the food or roller skating waiters? Please tell me you're not a rollerblader."

Detective Waters was fiddling with his food and didn't answer.

"Oh my God, you are, aren't you?"

"No, I'm not."

"Good. Want to hear a joke?"

"Sure," he said, still preoccupied with his thick shake.

She started laughing before she even began to tell it. "Okay, what's the hardest part about rollerblading?"

He didn't even try to think of an answer. "I don't know."

She grabbed his shoulder as if she had to brace him for the answer. "Telling your parents you're gay."

He grinned. She started laughing.

"That's not very PC, detective."

"I know." She downed a few fries. "When I was in the police academy, I was the only woman. They treated me like one of the guys and those were the only kind of jokes they told. Christ, I hope there were no gay guys in our group."

They laid their food out on the dashboard.

"Isn't this better than eating your lunch in the office and reading your gory websites?"

He nodded.

"See, getting these cases closed faster you can do stuff like this."

He took another drink from his shake, then turned to his partner. "So, why did you become a cop anyway?"

Wow, Chance Waters asked me a personal question.

"You sure you want to know? It's an odd story and takes some imagination."

"Sure."

"Okay. But no judging."

He agreed.

"Well, let's see. When I was twenty I tried mushrooms for the first—and only time." She looked at him. "The psychedelic kind, not portabellas."

"I assumed that," he said and reached for some of his fries.

"I was with a girlfriend. We were camping in the forest down in southern Illinois. It was part of my naturalist, living off the land phase. Mushrooms are natural, right? Can't hurt you. So, I wasn't that worried. We settled down for the night, started our campfire, cut up some shrooms and mixed them with lemon juice." She looked at Waters. "Someone told us they activate better that way. We sat back, prepared for the ride.

She looked at him, not sure what his reaction to her doing drugs would be. He seemed fine with it.

"About fifteen minutes passed, then something happened to me. I don't know what, I can't explain it. It was like a light switch was turned off.... or maybe on, I'm not sure, but it was weird."

She looked at her partner. He was listening intently.

"Then, the lights started flashing by, faster and faster. But I was in complete control, knew where I was, I wasn't panicky. Then, it stopped, and I was hovering above the earth, looking down at it, like in those pictures they take from the space station. I was just floating, watching for a while, then I start falling, slowly at first, then faster and faster. I saw Earth coming at me. I could see the ocean and continents in more detail, they were getting closer.

"I was heading towards America, out West somewhere, like Nevada or New Mexico, the desert states. Then I started to panic. I thought I was going to crash into the ground and die. Well, right before I hit, I came to a quick stop." She looked at her partner. "Still with me?"

He nodded.

"Here's where it gets weird...weirder. Imagine if what we know as reality is actually just a hazy, mid-level point. That there's a much deeper, clearer reality and awareness that we can tap into, and it's just outside of our grasp. All the confusing crap we don't understand normally, why things happen, it all becomes crystal clear. That's where I was. Sights were more vivid. Thoughts were more intense. Smells were more distinct. The air was cleaner and the sunset was a thousand times more colorful.

"So, I'm lying on my stomach in the desert, naked. The sun had just set and the sand was still warm. It felt great on my body." She looked at Waters. "That's it, no more dirty talk, don't worry."

"It was the most beautiful sunset ever. Combinations of reds and oranges spreading way out, not just on the horizon, you know that kind?"

Waters smiled and nodded.

"And I was never so aware of everything around me. I could see and hear and feel everything going on for miles away. And there weren't so many sensations that you get overwhelmed. And it was like I knew what was going to happen—like I'd already seen it.

"Then, I felt it, a presence coming near me, danger." She became more animated like she was reliving it. "I tried to move away from it, but I couldn't get up and walk. I tried to crawl, but couldn't lift my weight. I could feel it getting closer, then I could start to make out what it was."

She looked at Waters. "A big rattlesnake...I don't like snakes. Nothing on this planet scares me except snakes. So, it was coming closer, slithering toward me, and the odd part...I was afraid, but I knew it wasn't going to hurt me. It got right up to my face, about to strike, but it didn't. It didn't even rattle." She looked at him. "Isn't that weird?"

"Well, more and more rattlesnakes don't have rattles."

"What?"

"It's evolution. Ones that have rattles are getting killed by humans in those rattlesnake roundups and when they clear land. Their rattles give away their location and they get destroyed. Ones that don't rattle, survive, have babies."

She cocked her head. "Is that true?"

"Yes."

"Well, that's just great. I didn't need to know that. So, this rattlesnake, without a rattle, raised up like it was going to strike, but didn't. Then, his head turned into a muskrat's head, a friendly one, and it spoke. It said, 'Enjoy it while you can, girl. You're not going to make it past thirty'."

She looked at Waters. He was silent. "Well?" she said.

He thought for a moment. "How do you know it was a muskrat?"

"What do you mean?"

"All those animals look alike; muskrats, groundhogs, otters. How do you know it was a muskrat?"

"I just knew."

"So, you think you're going to die before you turn thirty?"

"Yes, absolutely. I think I'm already gone, what's about to happen has already been written."

"That's kind of sad."

"Depends on what's next."

"What do you mean?"

"Depends on what happens after this life. It could be better than this one, right? Lots of religions believe that."

"I guess so. And that's why you became a cop, to tempt fate?"

"No, I just made a promise to myself that night, if I was only going to live to thirty, I wasn't going to waste my time. I was never going to be bored. Never take a job that was boring. Never be with boring people. I took one year of college, got bored, left."

Waters gave her a puzzled look, she could tell he wasn't getting it.

"Being a cop is the most exciting job I've ever had, and it's probably the last thing anyone thought I would do. And you don't have to go to college for six years…and you get paid."

"I guess."

They both ate some more of their meal in silence. She could tell Waters was still trying to get a grasp on her life philosophy. "So, what about you? How did you become a detective?"

Waters finished the last of his hamburger, swallowed, and said, "I like puzzles."

Now she was confused. "And?"

"Detective work is the ultimate puzzle. It's a game, us against them, the smartest one wins."

"But you didn't start out as a detective."

"No, I was a beat cop for a while. Wasn't very good at it…even I realized that." She smiled at his rare display of self-awareness. "So, the chief had me assigned to the evidence room."

"Evidence room, yuck."

"I liked it. Everything in there is a puzzle piece. I started reading about the cases attached to the evidence items and solved some of the cases from them. Chief O'Halloran liked what I was doing and made me a detective. I was supposed to head up a mini forensic investigative unit, start focusing on some of the cold cases, but cutbacks ended that."

"Really? That's too bad." She thought about it for a second. "I bet you'd have been good at that. You like being a detective?" she asked and slipped her last pieces of french fries into her mouth.

"Some of it. It's mostly paperwork or sitting in the car watching people. I don't like those parts. But every once in a while you get an interesting case you can work."

They finished the rest of their lunch. Waters started the car, turned, and gave her a serious look. "Detective…if they ever make you take a psych exam, don't tell that story about the muskrat."

She smiled. "I won't."

CHAPTER 12

Two golf carts pulled up on the perfectly manicured path beside the green of the 18th hole of Ron Spiers' country club. Frank Thomas and Jacob Daniels got out of one cart, Ron Spiers and Shaun Williams got out of the other. They were all wearing the latest men's golf apparel, even their shorts were tailored to fit perfectly. They could have just stepped out of a men's fashion catalog.

"Last hole. This is for four hundred dollars ladies," Thomas informed his golfing partners as they made their way to their balls sitting on the green. They were playing teams, so there were only two golf balls in play.

"Okay, so if you guys par you win," Williams notified Thomas and Daniels, his opponents. "If Ron birdies, we win."

Ron Spiers stood over the ball, dead serious, concentrating on his eighteen-foot putt.

"Ron, do you breathe in or out when you putt?" Thomas asked right before he was about to hit the ball. The other two men laughed.

"I'll let you know after I sink this," he answered without looking up. He pulled the club back and made a textbook stroke. It rolled in a straight line toward the middle of the cup. At the last second, the ball veered right, hit the edge and lipped out.

Shaun Williams let out a loud groan—Daniels and Thomas smiled. Spiers clenched his jaw, picked up his ball, and threw it into the pond beside the green.

"That's all right, they still have to make this to tie," Williams consoled his partner.

Jacob Daniels had a pretty easy three-footer.

"That's in gimme range, no?" Thomas asked his opponents.

Spiers shot him a look that didn't require a response.

"Come on, Jacob, you got this," Thomas said to his partner.

Daniels looked nervous. He took a couple practice strokes, then lined up over the ball. His eyes looked down, then over to the cup, then down again.

Just before he started his stroke, Spiers spoke. "Jacob, if you make this, you're fired."

Daniels backed off the ball. Thomas and Williams laughed. Spiers and Daniels did not.

He returned to the ball, went through his routine again, then made his stroke. It missed badly to the left. Shaun Williams jumped up, let out a loud 'yes', and gave Ron Spiers a high five. Frank Thomas put the flag back in the hole and they returned to their carts.

***

The four men sat at a table at the 19th hole, the bar, with assorted mixed drinks in front of them. Jacob Daniels tallied up the score card, again. He looked at Spiers. "You birdied eight? That's the toughest hole on the course."

Spiers gave him a cocky nod.

"You're positive?"

"Three wood off the tee. Seven iron from one sixty to five feet of the pin. Putt center cup," Spiers replied and looked at Shaun Williams who gave a confirming head nod.

Daniels returned to the scorecard. "That's right then, they beat us by one," he informed Frank Thomas, his partner in the match.

Frank grabbed the scorecard and quickly totaled the number entered on each hole for both teams. "Yep, that's right." He tossed it to the center of the table towards Ron Spiers. "You want that for your scrap book?'

"Nah, this match shouldn't have been that close."

Thomas smiled.

"It's my fault, I missed two three-footers," Daniels said.

"No, it's mine. I was driving the ball like crap," Frank answered.

The waitress came over to the table. She was an attractive woman, probably mid-twenties "Another round of drinks?" she asked, looking directly at Ron Spiers.

He nodded.

She collected the empty glasses and left, giving Ron a lingering stare as she turned away.

"What's that all about," Shaun Williams asked Spiers.

"No idea," he said, not so convincingly.

"She's very pretty," Jacob Daniels added.

"Needs a little more upstairs," Shaun Williams replied.

"Big breasts are overrated," Ron chimed in.

"All you guys who have big boobs at home say that," Frank Thomas added.

"What do you like?" Spiers asked Frank.

He thought for a second. "I like a woman who's a good kisser."

The other guys laughed.

Thomas, not embarrassed at all, continued. "Seriously, kissing is very underrated. Think about it, how many times has it ruined a date, a girl who can't kiss. I bet Emma's a good kisser, right?" Frank asked looking at Ron.

"I'm not sure, why don't you ask Jacob," Ron said and looked at his understudy in the finance business.

Daniels blushed and didn't answer. The guys kept looking at him.

"How do you know how Emma kisses?" Shaun Williams finally asked.

Jacob looked at Ron Spiers. "Tell them," Spiers ordered him.

Daniels paused, then spoke. "We were over the other night, got a little drunk, started playing truth or dare. Ron dared me to make out with Emma."

"And you did?" Frank asked, half laughing, half stunned.

Daniels nodded.

"And, how was it?" Williams continued.

He looked at Spiers again before answering. "Very good."

"Victoria's a good kisser too," Ron added, giving Jacobs's wife a compliment.

"Jesus Christ, what's going on at that house?" Frank Thomas asked.

Spiers and Daniels smiled.

The waitress returned with the drinks. Spiers watched her place them in front of each of the men. She looked up at him as she finished.

"So, what's Jayne good at?" Spiers asked Frank Thomas.

He thought for a second. "Intense eyes. She knows how to look at you when being," he cleared his throat, "romantic."

They all looked at Shaun Williams. He smiled at the implicit query of what his wife Sky is good at. "Anything, anytime," he said and laughed.

"I'll drink to that," Jacob Daniels said and held up his glass for a toast. The guys lifted their glasses, clanged them together, and took a drink.

Ron Spiers chugged his and stood up. "All right, I have to get out of here. You guys got this?" He pushed the pad containing the tab over to Thomas and Daniels.

"Sure," Thomas said.

Shaun Williams stood up as well. "I have to go, too. See you guys Friday night."

He and Spiers gathered their things and headed to the parking lot.

"Want another drink? I don't have to be anywhere for an hour," Frank Thomas asked Daniels, the only two left.

"Sure."

Frank gave the waitress the two more hand signal. "So, how's work?"

"Busy. Always something going on down there. Making money, though."

"How's Ron to work for?"

"He's alright. Just don't make him look bad or cost him money and you'll be fine." Daniels said.

"How'd Ron make all his money, anyway?"

Daniels thought for a second, finished what was left of his drink, then leaned in toward Thomas like he didn't want anyone else to hear. "He made most of it in the nineties. He had a partner, they started a consulting firm. Made it big in the Internet boom."

"Really?"

"Yes. Then his partner died and Ron took over the business. Sold it a year later for millions."

"His partner died? How?"

"Suicide. Shot himself."

"Wow, that's tough"

"Yes. It was messy."

"What do you mean?"

"I don't know, lots of rumors flying around." The waitress stopped by with the drinks and Daniels stopped talking. She left and he continued. "Apparently the guy's widow didn't believe it. Tried to sue Ron for over a year. Then out of nowhere she just dropped the suit."

"She didn't believe it?"

"No, word is she said something else happened—that he would never have killed himself. He didn't even own a gun or know how to shoot one."

"Something else. Like what?"

Daniels shrugged. "No idea. Some people think Ron settled, paid her off, but required she never discuss it again, with anyone."

The two continued talking until they finished their drinks. The waitress came by and Frank Thomas handed her the bill and said, "Charge this to the Spiers account." She nodded. "And give yourself a fifty dollar tip."

The waitress smiled and took the check.

CHAPTER 13

Shaun Williams was getting in his early morning workout. He had a modest gym in the basement of his fashionable, upper middle-class home—mostly old school dumbbells and an elliptical machine.

After college Shaun became the finance manager at the Audi dealership. People liked him, he knew how to treat the wealthy customers and he understood the importance of repeat business. He was offered the general manager position when the owner retired.

He met his wife Sky at an annual gathering of top Dallas area minority business leaders, mostly black, a few Mexican. She was the facilitator of the meetings, one of the few women, and the only Caucasian to attend.

Shaun received the "Uncle Tom" treatment from some of the more contentious members of the group. It didn't help that he was so light complected and didn't speak the black street language when he was with the "brothas."

The TV was playing in the background and broadcasting the daily business reports. He sat on his bench press resting between sets; breathing heavily and sweating profusely. He was wearing athletic shorts, flip flops, and no shirt. He checked his reflection in the mirror and smiled. He was still in good shape.

Shaun stood and took a weight off each end of the bench press bar. They're easy to drop when people are tired, especially working out alone without a spotter. He laid back down on the bench, grabbed the bar, and lifted it off the rack. He did six reps, each one getting considerably more difficult. It was decision time to go for one more; he went for it.

He lowered the bar to his chest, closed his eyes, took a deep breath, then jerked it back up, barely able to extend his elbows. He went to put it back on the rack when something heavy landed on his chest, startling him.

It was his wife, Sky. She was straddling him, pinning him against the bench. She grabbed the bar, preventing him from putting it back on the rack. His elbows shook and the weight was balancing precariously over his head. He looked up at her.

"Don't drop it," she taunted him.

"Sky, stop."

"Come on, you can't hold it, you black pussy."

"Sky!"

His chest muscles twitched, he grimaced, then forced the bar back against her grip. It smacked loudly against the metal arms that held it above the bench.

"What the fuck," he said looking up at his hot strawberry blonde of a wife. She had fair skin and a shapely body. She was more sexy than pretty.

Her tits were barely being held back by her loose fitting tank top. She had an intense look in her eyes, holding him down with all her weight concentrated on his chest, her knees by his ears. The bottom of her shirt hung over his face. He glimpsed under it and realized she wasn't wearing any panties.

"Christ," he said, and let out a nervous laugh; probably more out of relief he didn't have a two hundred pound bench press across his face.

"You like that?" she said in a low aggressive voice.

He grinned and nodded.

"Yeah, you like that. Then lick it." She slid her crotch from his chest to his chin.

"Get that tongue out," she said and drove her hips closer toward his head. Her pussy was pressed against his chin. He was performing oral on her whether he wanted to or not.

"Yeah, get that tongue in there, lick it."

She pressed her tightly shaved bush against his face, quickening the motion of her hips. She lifted herself up off his chest, then grabbed his hand and guided it between her legs. "Get that thumb in there. Now, you little bitch."

He did as he was told.

"Yeah, right there—rub it." She started to moan. "Tongue that clit, now, you little bitch," she said, competing with the sound of the business reporter on the TV. "Now get those shorts off."

He reached down with his free hand and pulled off his shorts and underwear, lifting them over his stiff penis. She slid down from his chest to his waist. His hand came out from under her and she raised her hips and began sliding her pussy on top of his penis, not letting it penetrate her.

"You like that?"

He nodded.

"Yeah, I can tell, you like that." She reached down and guided his penis inside her, just a little at first, teasing him, holding herself above him. "How does that feel?"

"Good," he said in a low voice.

She started moving slowly, riding him with her hips, finally allowing him to slide all the way in. She leaned over and whispered in his ear, "Yeah, that feels good, doesn't it? My tight pussy around your huge cock."

He started to move faster, lifting his hips up and down to meet hers. She reached down, pulled him out of her and grabbed him tightly around the base of his cock. "Don't you come, you hear me? Not yet!"

"I'm trying," he said, his face showing the competing emotions of agony and pleasure.

She released his penis, grabbed hold of the base of his sack, and squeezed his testicles. "You hear me? Hold it or I'll rip your nuts off."

"I am," he said, his face in full grimace now. She was still grinding her hips against him, his penis rubbing against her ass.

"Hold it, come on, make it last."

"I'm trying." Too late, he ejaculated all over her back side.

"Dammit," she said and climbed off him, releasing his groin. She took off her tank top and used it to wipe off her bottom.

She looked down at him, his arms and legs hanging lifeless off the sides of the bench press. "You need to do better," she said and headed back upstairs.

CHAPTER 14

Chance Waters walked through the doors of a busy Sports Bar. His eyes darted from table to table as he tried to see around the hostess who was asking him questions.

He agreed to meet Detective McBayne out for dinner, even surprising himself by accepting the invitation. It already appeared to have been a big mistake. He turned to leave, stopped, then turned back around.

Waters scanned the restaurant but couldn't see a table with a lone woman—a confident, self-assured woman who seemed comfortable in any situation, with anyone, the complete opposite of him. He looked at the bar, nothing.

Walking down a hallway towards the bathroom someone called to him. "Waters, over here." It was his partner's voice.

Detective McBayne sat at a table with five men. The remains of food on appetizer plates, empty pitchers, and partially filled glasses littered the table. He approached the group, focusing on her face.

"Detective Waters, these are my old cop pals." She motioned to the guys around the table and made introductions. None of the names or faces were familiar except Perry Jackson, the older black fellow to McBayne's right.

"Pull up a seat, detective, join us," Perry said.

Waters hesitated, looked toward the bathroom, then the front door. He glanced at his partner—she gave him an inviting smile and the sorry about that smile. He sat at the open spot across from her.

"These guys were supposed to be gone an hour ago, but they get to drinking and tend to overstay their welcome," McBayne said. A couple "oohs" from the men acknowledging the subtle slight. "They probably think I'm paying, too."

"You are making the big bucks now, Detective McBayne," one of the cops said, stressing the word Detective.

"We can't leave a lady sitting here drinking by herself, now can we? This is a dangerous city for a defenseless little girl," another officer said sarcastically and took a swig of his beer. The others smiled.

"Is this a date, should we leave?" the same cop asked.

McBayne shook her head, no response from Waters.

"Would you like a beer?" Perry asked Waters and lifted the pitcher.

"No, I'm fine."

"Wow, that's the first time one of McPain's acquaintances ever turned down a drink," one of the cops said. The others laughed. They were all well on their way to being intoxicated, making every comment more entertaining than it really was.

"McPain?" Waters said, realizing the officer mispronounced her name.

"That's what we called her when she was a lowly cop," a stocky blonde headed officer at the end of the table said. "A lot of her suspects seemed to show up at the precinct roughed up a bit." He looked at McBayne. "How's the anger management coming, McPain?"

"I don't know, how's the premature ejaculation coming, Stinson?" McBayne said. All the other cops started laughing, even Stinson.

Carlie turned to her partner. "Waters, Perry was one of my trainers at the police academy," she said and gave the man beside her a pat on the shoulder. "Taught me everything I know."

Waters nodded. She had mentioned him a few times since they'd been partners. She seemed to admire him.

"Yep, she was a shy little thing when I got her. Look at her now. A big shot detective."

"How many pimps and drug dealers has she beaten the crap out of, Detective," another cop asked Waters.

He looked at McBayne as if he'd missed something. "None."

"Give her time. No one hates dealers more than her."

"Just the ones who sell to kids," McBayne spoke up in her defense.

The waiter came by and asked the group if they needed more beer. McBayne gave him a definitive "no" and explained that they were leaving as soon as they finished their drinks. Waters ordered a club soda with lemon.

The group of cops continued their conversation, which was mostly retold stories from previous experiences with each other and Detective McBayne. She filled in the blanks and background stories for him when necessary.

Finally, one of the officers addressed him directly. "Detective Waters, do you remember me?"

Waters looked at him, thought for a second, then shook his head.

"You were called to a disturbance on the South side one time. I was one of the officers on the scene."

Another Waters' head shake.

The cop started telling the story to the entire table. "So, we get a call to the home of a legendary Cowboy's wide receiver. I can't state his name, but his initials were..." He listed the initials and the table confirmed they knew who he was talking about. Waters had no idea.

"This guy had a party at his house, well, his mansion. It got out of control—a fight broke out and one of the guests got the living shit kicked out of them. So, Detective Waters shows up with his partner to investigate. Per usual, no one would talk. The Detective inspected the entire compound, took pictures of everything, including the player's shoes." The cop laughed to himself. "Well, this guy thinks the Detective is just a fan trying to get close to him and get memorabilia and pictures. But you had no idea who he was, did you, detective?"

Waters shook his head.

"I didn't think so. So, anyway, all the evidence the Detective gathered cleared the player of any wrongdoing. He even took pictures of the bottom of the player's shoes. Turns out, his footprint didn't match any of the prints in the dirt where the victim got his ass kicked."

Waters looked at his partner. She smiled at him.

The cop continued the story. "A few days later, a big box arrives at the precinct for him." He looked at Detective Waters, nothing. "Inside is a signed football, a picture of the player that says, 'Thank you, Detective Waters', new cleats and a bunch of other stuff. The mail guy at the station put it on the Detectives desk." He looked at Waters. "Do you remember what you did with it?"

Waters thought for a moment. "I think I threw it out."

"Yes, you did."

"We're not supposed to accept gifts," Waters said.

The group laughed, until they realized he was serious.

"How the hell did you know what he did with it?" McBayne asked.

"Because, I'm the one who fished it out of the trash room. I took the football home and gave it to my son."

"Not a big Cowboys fan, Detective?" Perry asked him.

Waters shook his head.

"Thank you for that Detective. It's still one of the best birthday presents my boy ever got." He raised his glass toasting Detective Waters.

"All right men, let's wrap it up and let these two have their dinner," Perry informed the group.

The men finished their beers and stood. They all threw some cash into a pile on the table. Perry slid it over to Detective McBayne. "This should take care of it, if not let me know."

She nodded.

"Nice meeting you, Detective. Take care of our girl," Perry said and reached out and shook Waters' hand.

As the officers left, McBayne moved to a seat next to her partner. "Sorry about that, they were supposed to be gone after the game." She made a motion to the TV above their table.

"That's okay," Waters said.

They ordered their food and continued talking. Some personal stuff—some police work.

Detective Waters looked across the table at his partner. "Why do you hate drug dealers so much?"

She thought for a second, took a drink of her beer, then said, "Because, they killed my friend."

Waters looked at her, puzzled.

"It's a long story."

CHAPTER 15

Dr. Charles Browning was out back by the pool, sitting with his feet up on one of the poolside chairs. He had a mojito on the end table beside him and was checking the news on his iPad. He wore a white bathrobe, having just swum a few laps in the nude.

His house was big and gaudy, with a four car garage, and they only had two cars. One bay was occupied by a large lawn tractor that had never been driven—he had a service that took care of the lawn. They had the best of everything, including a twenty-five hundred dollar espresso machine imported from Italy.

The doctor grew up in Northern California and attended Cal Berkley as an undergrad, then went to Baylor College of Medicine in Houston. He was the preeminent heart surgeon in the Dallas-Ft. Worth area. He had a nineteen-year-old son who lived with the first Mrs. Browning.

His second wife, Charlene, was better than most stunningly attractive second wives, especially considering he met her at a boat show. She was one of the models used to attract wealthy men to the luxury yachts. Charlene was in her final year at a community college studying accounting when they met. She even did the books for the modeling agency.

She rarely embarrassed him with young, trophy wife silliness. She got propositioned by his rich friends and colleagues at nearly every function they attended, but he seemed more flattered than bothered by it.

The door of the back porch opened and Charlene walked out wearing a thin black bikini—she looked fantastic. She approached her husband and stopped at the end of his chair. He looked up, smiled, and put his iPad on the table. She let him enjoy the view for a while—just about anyone would buy a boat from this woman.

She playfully rubbed her hands over her body, pushed her tits together, then slid her hand down past her belly button. She parted her legs and her fingers disappeared into the front of her bikini. She began to moan as if just looking at him was getting her off.

She did that for a few seconds, then moved closer and straddled his chair, her crotch positioned directly in front of his face. She took off her top exposing her perfect, unaltered breasts. She leaned down and let them hang in front of his face.

"You like these?"

He nodded and reached out to feel them.

"Not yet. No touching." She let them dangle in front of his face a bit longer, teasing him. "Do you want to come on them?"

Another nod from Charles, although that was probably a rhetorical question.

"Are you ready?"

"Yes," the doctor said and flung open his robe, and he was ready.

"I'm going to sit on that huge cock. Are you sure you can handle it?"

She glanced at her watch, sat beside him, and started stroking his penis—looking him right in the eye the entire time. She moved her face toward his, their lips almost touching, and stopped just before making contact. He closed his eyes and his head rolled back.

She stroked him for about a minute, looked at her watch again, then stopped and stood up. He slid down on the chair until he was almost laying on his back. She maneuvered herself on top of him, leaned over, and placed his penis between her tits. She pushed them together and started moving up and down.

He started to moan deeper now, moving his hips in rhythm with her. She continued for another minute then stopped and slid down, removed his penis from between her tits, and placed her face over his groin, teasing him.

Finally, she took him into her mouth. He looked down at her then leaned his head back and closed his eyes. He started moaning uncontrollably, let out one last groan, grabbed the back of her head, and pulled her towards him as far as she would go. "Aw, fuck," he said and ejaculated.

She remained where she was for a few seconds until he recovered, then sat up on the end of the chair. She grabbed a towel from the table beside him, spit into it, and wiped her mouth.

She looked at her watch, then down at him and said, "Emma Spiers is going to eat you alive, Charlie."

She turned, took two large steps, and dove into the swimming pool.

CHAPTER 16

It was Friday evening, just past ten o'clock, Waters and McBayne were the on-call detectives that evening. They'd been dispatched to a house in Southlake. A man had reportedly taken a fall and died.

Finally, some real action, detective McBayne thought to herself as her partner turned his blue Ford down an old country road. Every house in the neighborhood was big and beautiful with three and four-acre lots, impeccable landscaping, pools, large open decks, and gate entries with camera's and intercoms.

This was where the elite of the elite in the Dallas-Ft. Worth area lived. Originally it was home to the pioneers in the oil boom of the seventies, but now it was high tech, medical, and finance industry tycoons. All their children went to private school; there wasn't even school bus service in this neighborhood. It was fairly dark outside, but they could still see the magnitude of the houses from the lights and driveway entrances.

Detective McBayne looked out her window. "Holy shit, I didn't even know this neighborhood existed."

"Yeah, we don't get many calls out here. It's just the wealthy and people who work for the wealthy."

They drove a little farther and approached the sprawling Spiers estate on the left. Directly across the street was another spread just as impressive. It had a for sale sign out front that looked more like a sign for a fancy Inn. The house was daunting, like a haunted house sitting on a hill with no lights on.

"Hey, Detective, there's a house for sale if you need a new place," McBayne informed her partner.

They turned into the Spiers' driveway. Like most of them, it circled the entire front yard and had an elegant walkway and sitting area in the middle that was probably only used by the landscape workers to have lunch. A police cruiser and an ambulance were already parked out front. As they made their way up the driveway, they could see people upstairs on the elaborate balcony with ivy growing around it.

Waters pulled up beside the cruiser and stopped. They made their way up the stone stairway and entered through the glass front door. It opened into a large, beautiful, circular entry way with mahogany wood decorating the walls. It was a stunning entrance that immediately let their guests know, yes, we're doing quite well.

"Wow, welcome to the Hotel California," McBayne said as she walked through the doorway and looked around.

Waters gave her a confused look. "We're in Texas."

"Never mind."

Twin staircases started at the hallway ahead of them and made their way in opposite directions, ascending both sides of the room to the second floor. Expensive artwork adorned the walls the entire length of each staircase. Straight ahead, through a short hallway, was a living room with ridiculously high ceilings. Standing on the right side of the entry was one of the policemen who greeted them as they approached.

"Detectives, I'm Officer Little. Officer Clement is upstairs with the EMT's."

They nodded.

"We received a nine-one-one call around nine fifteen this evening from the owner of the house, a Mr. Ronald Spiers. He and his wife were having drinks with another couple." He looked at his notebook, "Jayne and Frank Thomas. Mr. Thomas is the deceased. He's upstairs on the front balcony." The officer motioned above their heads where the stairs circled around.

"Mr. and Mrs. Spiers and Mrs. Thomas are in the living room," he said and looked down the hallway between the two staircases.

"Okay, thank you, Officer. Anything else," Waters asked him.

"No. Seems pretty straightforward—drunk guy takes a fall and cracks his head open. No sign of a struggle."

"All right." Waters turned his attention to Detective McBayne. "Why don't you interview those three. I'll check out the accident scene."

***

McBayne headed down the hallway to the living room. Ron Spiers was standing with his back turned, looking out one of the floor to ceiling windows overlooking his back yard. Two women sat at each end of a couch. Completely preoccupied, they didn't notice the detective enter the room. Spiers turned as she approached and addressed her.

"Hello, Officer."

"It's Detective, McBayne," she corrected him.

"Right, Detective. I'm Ron Spiers, this is my home." He motioned to the woman at the far end of the couch. "That's Mrs. Thomas. Her husband is the one who had the accident."

"How's she doing?"

"Okay, considering."

"And this is your wife?"

"Yes, that's Emma."

"Can you tell me what happened, Mr. Spiers?" she asked and took a small notebook pad and pen from her back pocket.

"Sure." He paused to collect his thoughts. "Let's see, the Thomas's arrived shortly after seven for cocktails. They're two of our closest friends. We were here in the living room, talking. About an hour later Frank and I went upstairs to get some fresh air on the balcony." He pointed upstairs. "He and I talked for a while, then I went back downstairs to freshen our drinks."

McBayne took notes as he spoke.

"On my way back upstairs I heard a thud, then a loud crash. When I got to the balcony, Frank was lying on the floor, bleeding from his head, unresponsive. He must have fallen and hit his head on the wine table up there. It's knocked over."

"Did you notice anything peculiar about him tonight? Was he acting strange, disoriented?"

Spiers leaned in toward the detective, glanced at Jayne Thomas, then spoke in a lower voice. "Well, he was drinking more than usual. I've noticed tension between them the last few weeks. But other than that, nothing."

"What were you talking about?" McBayne asked.

"Um, just normal stuff; work, golf, the Cowboys. Nothing exciting. He and Jayne were planning a cruise; Alaska, I think he said. Emma and I have done that trip before, so we were giving them some ideas."

"Okay, thank you, Mr. Spiers. Let me know if you can think of anything else."

He nodded.

Detective McBayne walked over to Mrs. Thomas, put her hand on her shoulder, and sat down.

***

The twin staircases met the second floor at opposite sides of the room. It opened into a large sitting area that was set up almost like a mini arena. The room contained a couch, love seat, and two wide chairs surrounding a large round leather ottoman—it looked out of place with the Victorian age style furniture.

Everything in the room was positioned to provide a stunning view through the doors. Four elegant glass doors lead outside to the balcony overlooking the front of the estate with the driveway just beneath it.

Officer Clement stood at attention in the open doorway to the right. A cool, early spring breeze entered the house through the doors. The deceased, Frank Thomas, was positioned on his back on the left side of the balcony. A large puddle of blood surrounded his upper body and a nasty wound was visible on the side of his head. He looked peaceful like he was sleeping. A small side table with a granite top and thin wrought iron legs was laying on its side just beyond him, about fifteen feet away.

Detective Waters scanned the scene, taking particular note of the table. It didn't look very practical and couldn't hold more than a couple glasses and a bottle of wine.

Two EMT's sat on a stretcher out of the way. They looked preoccupied. One was checking his email on his phone, the other appeared to be singing to himself and trying to remember the lyrics to a song.

Detective Waters knelt on one knee, taking pictures of the accident scene. He twisted his body and took more shots from a slightly different angle. He stood—his eyes panning the room as he stepped off the distance from the balcony wall to the now departed Mr. Thomas, making sure not to step in the puddle of blood.

The detective took pictures from every angle of the upturned table. He stood on a spot near the accident victim's feet and looked out from the balcony to the property in front. He walked back to the doors, stopped, took one more picture, and turned his attention to the EMT's. "Okay, let's get the crime lab up here."

He hit one of the speed dials on his phone, put it to his ear, and waited for an answer. "Hello, this is Detective Waters at the residence of Ron Spiers. We need a crime lab on the scene." He listened for a few seconds. "Umm, I really think we need one to come out. There're some oddities about the scene."

Another pause from Waters. "Okay, no crime lab." He hit the end button on his phone.

The EMT's looked at each other and appeared happy. Waiting for CSI to arrive and complete their work would take hours. Waters addressed the two men. "That's good then, you can take him."

The technician on the phone spoke. "No CSI, Detective?"

"They won't send them out. Not to this neighborhood on a Friday night for a probable accident."

The detective left the balcony and started taking pictures of the sitting room. He continued his photo session as he descended the opposite staircase making his way back down to the main entrance. He passed through the hallway and into the living room where Detective McBayne was now talking with Mrs. Spiers. Ron Spiers watched him closely as he meticulously inspected the entire room, continuing to take photos.

"Did anyone move the deceased or touch anything on the balcony?" he asked the group in general.

"No," Spiers said and glanced at the two women for their response.

"I held Frank's head and kissed him," Mrs. Thomas said. She held out her hands showing dried blood on her arms and the front of her green dress. She started crying again.

Waters raised his phone and snapped pictures of the woman and the blood stains.

"All right, that's enough," Mr. Spiers said. "Is this necessary?"

"Did you touch him, too?" Waters asked Emma Spiers, pointing to blood on her dress.

She looked up at the detective. "I might have. I don't remember."

He leaned down and took pictures of her bloodstains.

"Are you almost done, Detective?" Spiers asked. "This woman's husband just died. She's devastated, and I need to get her home."

"Is the kitchen this way?" Waters asked and headed down the hallway, not waiting for a response.

"Yes, that should wrap things up. We'll finish and be on our way," Detective McBayne assured Mr. Spiers. She turned and followed her partner down the hallway toward the kitchen.

Waters completed his inspection of the rest of the house. The EMT's brought the stretcher downstairs, careful not to hit the expensive wood paneling. The Spiers and Mrs. Thomas stood in the hallway watching them take Frank away.

"We'll be filing a report in the next few days. I'll get a copy to both of you," MacBayne said to Spiers and Mrs. Thomas. "Can I get your cell numbers, we'll need to contact you?"

She held out her notebook and pen. Spiers took them and jotted down the numbers.

"Again, I'm sorry for your loss, Mrs. Thomas," McBayne said and touched her gently on the back of her shoulder. The officers and detectives followed the EMT's out of the house.

Waters stopped in the driveway before they got to the car. He looked up at the balcony and took a few more pictures with the flash on. He looked to the left, right, the front of the mini mansion, and the rest of the yard, taking pictures of each area. He turned, looked down the driveway to the house for sale across the street. McBayne watched him curiously.

"All right, let's go," he said.

They got into their car and followed the driveway as it circled around and headed back out the front gate and down the country road the way they came.

"Well, what do you think?" McBayne asked her partner.

He thought for a second. "Something's not right about the accident scene."

"What do you mean?"

"The position of the body and that table."

"Mrs. Thomas did say she held him. Maybe she moved him and didn't realize."

"I need to analyze the photos. We'll see."

"What do you think?" he asked her in a rare, unprompted query.

"What do I think....If your best friend's husband just died, would you be sitting at the end of the couch away from her?"

Already Gone

Waters wasn't sure what she was getting at, of course, human nature wasn't his specialty, inanimate objects were.

"You'd be sitting beside her, comforting her. I agree, something doesn't seem right."

CHAPTER 17

"The Jones-Hernandez case is almost closed out," Detective McBayne informed the chief. "Just need the summary report filed. Costco break-in is a dead end. We handed the Park Side shooting over to Detective Watson. It's definitely a gang hit, and it will go unsolved like the rest of them."

The chief gave her the "of course" nod.

"My old contacts on the street are all dried up. They know I'm not around anymore, so no leverage." She glanced at her notes. "And, that's it."

"Very good." The chief looked at Waters, who'd been sitting silently. "See how she did that, Detective? Quick, clear, concise."

"Yes sir, I did."

"Three cases cleared in less than a week. That's what we're looking for. You two are becoming a solid team." He shot an approving nod to his two detectives. "Okay, the Thomas death. I read your report. What's the latest?"

Waters answered. "Well, sir, we're just getting started. I'm still doing some analysis, but preliminary findings, I don't think it was an accident. Or at least not the way they reported it."

"Why not?"

"The accident scene. It's not right. I don't think he fell."

"Why?"

"Well, there's the obvious. The head wound is on the side, not the front or back, indicating a blow, not a fall. And I'm pretty sure the objects on that balcony were moved."

"What objects?"

"The body, the wine table, maybe both."

"Interesting. Why didn't you get the lab in there?"

"I called. They wouldn't come out."

"They wouldn't come out? A detective called for CSI and they said no?"

Waters shrugged.

"Who did you talk to?"

"I don't know, whoever was at the board Friday evening."

The chief thought for a second. "Well, Waters, you do tend to call CSI if a cat gets stuck in a tree, but that still isn't right. I'll try to find out what happened. We still need some hard evidence, doesn't look like that will be forthcoming?"

"Maybe. I'm still analyzing the data."

"What data? I thought you said there was no CSI?"

"There wasn't, but I took a lot of pictures."

The chief laughed. "You took a lot of pictures, did you? You remember to get a selfie with the dead guy?" He looked at Detective McBayne. She smiled in fake amusement.

"And you?" he asked, keeping his attention on his female investigator.

"I agree, sir. I think Spiers is lying."

"Why?"

"I just do."

"And?"

"And what?" McBayne asked.

"That's it, you just *do*. Because you *think so*." He glanced at Waters, then back to McBayne. "You know what? I think I want to be a porn star, I just do. But that's not going to make it so."

McBayne let out a nervous laugh.

"Something funny about that, Detective?"

"No, sir, I think you'd make an excellent porn star."

"Well, thank you, I do as well."

He focused his gaze on the lady detective and spoke like a professor making a critical point to a student. "Ms. McBayne, detective work is about facts and evidence, not thoughts and feelings." His attention turned back to both of them. "All right. So, no motive, no hard evidence, no one caught in a lie?" He paused, they nodded. "It's Friday morning, you've been on this a week and that's it?" He waited for a response, nothing. "Time to close it down, Detectives. Move on to the next case."

A moment of silence, then Waters spoke up. "Well, there is the issue of the missing glasses."

McBayne looked at him.

"According to Detective McBayne's notes, Mr. Spiers said he went to get drinks for himself and Mr. Thomas when the accident happened. He was on his way back upstairs when he heard the crash. He said he went to the victim, tried to help him, but he was already dead."

"And?" the chief asked, presumably having no idea what he was getting at.

McBayne was looking at him very interested as well.

"Where did the glasses go?"

"Hmmm," the chief said, "you didn't find them anywhere?"

"No, I searched the whole house, nothing. The sink and dishwasher were empty, no wet glasses in the cabinet or even a damp dish towel."

"Well, the wife could have cleaned it up. Some people do that, especially under duress." He looked at Detective McBayne. "Did she say she cleaned up the place?"

"Umm, no. She said she didn't do a thing. Sat on the couch waiting for the EMT's."

"Okay, that'll buy you a couple more days. But if nothing comes up, we're moving on. Got it?"

Waters nodded.

"You have until the end of day Tuesday. If that's it, let's get back to work."

The detectives left the chief's office. As soon as the door shut McBayne got in Detective Water's face. She didn't look happy.

"Waters, what the fuck," she said, trying to yell at him without drawing attention.

"What?"

"You made me look like an ass in there."

He had no idea what she was talking about.

"Why didn't you tell me about the glasses? You find a major clue, in my goddamn notes even, and you don't mention it?"

"I thought it was obvious."

"I looked like an idiot in there. *I just do, Chief,*" she said, mocking herself. She shook her head. "We're supposed to be a team, right?"

He nodded.

"That's the kind of shit we tell each other. Christ, Waters, crap like that is why you can't keep a partner."

She turned and headed off toward the break room. He returned to his cube—still not sure what he did wrong.

***

The detectives continued working throughout the morning. McBayne went over her notes from beginning to end to see what else she might have missed. She was as much embarrassed for missing the glasses clue as she was pissed at Waters for not informing her.

She also didn't know the theory about the head injury being on the side indicating it wasn't a fall. She'd been doing a good job in her detective role so far, but this shook her confidence. It was the first case she had that required real detective work, not common sense and brute force, which was her specialty.

She logged into her computer and browsed to a server where Waters uploaded all the pictures he took at the scene. She started reviewing them. There were hundreds of photos, many of the same scene from a slightly different angle. It was going to take hours to go over them all.

Detective Waters was at his desk beside her. She noticed him peeking over his cube wall every few minutes, looking like he wanted to talk. She ignored him as long as she could until she couldn't take it any longer.

She turned to look at him. "What?"

"Are you still mad at me?" he asked.

She couldn't help but let out an exasperated laugh. "Yes, I'm mad. We're not B-F-F's anymore and I'm unfriending you on Facebook."

"I'm not on Facebook."

Another futile laugh. "I'm not pissed, just don't do that crap again. We're partners, we tell each other everything, even if you think it's obvious. Right?"

He slowly nodded in agreement and now had an even more tormented look on his face. "Okay." He looked around as if he was making sure no one was listening, leaned closer to her, and whispered. "I have to show you something."

She leaned toward their shared cube wall, imitating him and whispered back in a mocking tone, "What?"

"It's at my apartment."

"You want to go to your apartment now?"

He thought for a second. "No, we better not. Someone might see us. How about tonight after work, around seven?"

"Sure." She returned to her work.

"Hey," he said followed by another lean in and whisper. "Can we make it eight? I have yoga tonight."

"Fine." Under her breath, she commented to no one in particular. "That's not creepy at all."

"What?"

"Nothing."

CHAPTER 18

Detective McBayne pulled her six-year-old Ford Mustang into an open spot in front of Waters' building. She bought it the week she became a cop and started receiving consistent paychecks.

Detective Waters lived in a plain looking building with only six units. His was on the middle floor to the right. She approached the front door and wondered if she was the first woman to ever visit Waters at home.

It was obvious the resident name labels weren't up to date nor were the intercom buttons working. The building had the distinct feel that it contained an odd assortment of inhabitants; probably all of varying backgrounds, such as a thirty-three-year-old single police detective with undefined sexual preference who might just be a genius hermit.

She pushed on the heavy glass door. It resisted, but finally opened. She climbed the stairs and was standing in front of Waters' apartment, number 203. The detective put her ear against the door, not sure what she was listening for. She knocked while discreetly putting her hand under her jacket near her pistol, more out of habit than anything else.

Waters opened the door. "Hi, come in." He turned and walked back into the apartment.

She poked her head in and looked around. It was dark and her eyes hadn't adjusted yet. She followed him into the room as the smell of mild spices hit her, some combination of cinnamon or nutmeg, maybe a hint of chocolate.

"How was yoga class?" she asked as her eyes scanned her partner's dwelling.

"Really good. My favorite instructor was there," he said cheerfully.

"Oh great." She was expecting a quick, undescriptive one-word answer like "fine." Waters rarely offered more information than needed.

Waters residence was a basic bachelor's apartment, neater than most. There was not, however, the obvious man-cave accessories, like beer lights, sports memorabilia, or a makeshift bar—and she didn't expect there to be. To the right, the living room consisted of a couch, chair, and coffee table, but no TV. It didn't look as if the room got a lot of use. On her left was the kitchen. It was sparsely furnished as well, nothing on the counter tops except a coffee pot, two mugs, and a large silver thermos. A small glass table and three cheap wicker chairs finished the décor of the room.

"No TV? Or are you a bedroom TV watcher?"

He turned to face her. "No, I don't watch TV."

"Well, that explains a lot," she said and smiled.

No reaction from Waters. Apparently he didn't realize, or probably care, that his complete ignorance of pop culture was peculiar.

The hallway ahead to the right presumably led to the bedrooms and bathroom.

A bright light from the dining room ahead on the left caught her eye. She took a couple steps toward the room, glancing toward Waters. He nodded, giving her approval to move closer. As she approached it became clearer what she was looking at.

Three large, flat screen monitors were placed side by side on top of an old wooden desk like an accountant from 1945 would have. There was a matching wooden swivel chair in front of it. The modern technology and antique furniture made an interesting contrast. Two computers at each end of the desk powered the monitors, which were providing most of the light in the apartment. On top of the computers was a router and other supporting devices with blinking lights. She stepped up to the desk and looked closer at the displays.

She stared for a few moments, eyeing each of the monitors, then started to comprehend what she was looking at. She turned to Waters who was standing beside her now.

"Holy shit, when did you do this?"

"I do it for all of my more complex cases."

Spanning the screens were several different colored blocks arranged in concentric circles with solid and dashed lines joining them. In the middle was a red block with a picture of Frank Thomas under the label "VICTIM."

Under Frank's picture was a thorough and detailed list of information about him, including spouse, residences, colleges, profession, employers, salary, vehicles, hobbies, acquaintances, criminal offenses, traffic violations, bank accounts, payments, purchases, deposits, and other personal information. Each data item was an underlined link presumably to click on for more information. There was a small number in parenthesis if multiple entries existed, like 'Traffic Violation (4).'

Beside Frank's block was a dark blue one containing a picture of his wife, Jayne Thomas, with the title "SUSPECT." Below her picture was the same information categories as Frank's. There was additional data at the bottom of her section that said 'Alibi' with a value of 'None', 'Opportunity' was set to 'Yes', and 'Motive' had a question mark.

Connecting Frank and Jayne's blocks was a solid line which said, 'Relationship: Wife.'

Beside Jayne's block was another dark blue one divided vertically in two. It contained Ron and Emma Spier's pictures and all the info about them below it. The solid line connecting them to Frank's said, 'Relationship: Friend.'

There were three more image blocks surrounding Frank's. They contained different couple's names and photos. Each had the same information sections and connecting lines, but with varying shades of blue. Some of the relationship lines were dashes instead of solid lines. Detective McBayne didn't recognize the other three couple's names or faces.

"Who are these people?" she said and went to touch one of them on the screen.

Waters grabbed her hand. "Don't touch it."

Startled, and surprised at being touched by Waters, she said, "Why? What will happen?"

"You'll leave fingerprints."

"Oh."

He handed her a small wand. It was a little larger than a pencil with a round plastic tip. "Use this."

Waters sat in the swivel chair and rolled it under the desk in front of the monitors. McBayne knelt beside him. He grabbed the mouse and started pointing to the different items on the screen. "This is our victim, Frank Thomas, and everything we know about him. The dark blue boxes immediately adjacent are known acquaintances. The darker the shade of blue, the higher degree of a suspect. Spouse is always the main suspect unless she has a rock solid alibi."

He held the mouse over the relationship line that said 'Wife' for Mrs. Thomas. A text box popped up with personal information about how they met. He pointed to the data on the screen. "So, Frank and Jayne Thomas met in 2008 at this publishing company. She was a junior editor, just out of college—SMU. He was her supervisor. They got married two years later. No kids. This link…" He clicked the link and a map popped up on the screen. "Takes you to a map showing their residence. It also has the latest Google satellite images."

Detective McBayne turned her head from the monitors to her partner. His persona had suddenly changed from the awkward, self-conscious man, to a confident, highly capable computer expert explaining complex items on a computer display. There was the added intrigue of how he obtained this data.

McBayne looked at him. "Wait a minute, are you one of those hackers. Is this illegal?"

Waters thought for a moment. "No…and probably not."

He continued. "The Spiers, also in dark blue because of their high suspect probability, are obviously linked from the crime scene being at their house, but also by their relationship."

He dragged the mouse over the 'Friend' relationship line between Thomas and Spiers. A text box appeared that said, 'Met at HeadStart fundraiser in Dallas' and the date of the event, three months earlier.

McBayne was quiet as she tried to take in all the information. She went to touch another block on the screen with her finger. Waters gave her a look and motioned toward the pointer. She picked it up.

"So, who are the rest of these people?" she said and pointed to a block that said 'Jacob and Victoria Daniels.'

Waters moved the mouse over the solid relationship line between Spiers and Daniels. It said 'Colleagues.' A popup appeared showing they worked together at Taylor Financial and the day Jacob Daniels started.

"So, why is he solid blue? He's a suspect just from working with Spiers?"

Waters looked at her. "Good question."

He clicked on the "Payments" link under Jacob Daniels' info section. A separate window appeared with a list of what looked like financial transactions. One item midway down was highlighted.

McBayne read it. "Debit card payment for seventy-eight dollars to Total Beer and Wine."

She looked at Waters. "And?"

"Look at the date. Last Friday, seven-fourteen pm."

McBayne struggled to make the connection. "Okay, so it was the day Frank died, about an hour before. But how is it related to the accident?"

Waters clicked on a small map icon beside the transaction. Another screen appeared containing a map with three highlighted locations. One was the Daniels residence with a small icon and his face. A few inches away, equaling several miles on the map, were two more locations side by side. One was the Spiers house and had Ron's picture. The other was the Total Beer and Wine store where the purchase was made.

McBayne continued thinking out loud. "So, Daniels made a purchase at the Wine store several miles from their house, but just down the road from the Spiers', last Friday, an hour before the accident."

It hit her. She turned and looked at Waters. "You think they were there that night?"

Her partner nodded. "Well, the data suggests a high probability. And look at the other highlighted transactions, several purchases at the same wine store, all on Friday, all about the same time."

Waters moved the mouse to another block. "Same with these two couples, Shaun and Sky Williams and Charles and Charlene Browning. They're lighter blue because the connection isn't as strong. A dashed line means it's not a direct relationship, probably friends of friends. Sky Williams used an ATM near the Spiers house almost every Friday, same time, just after seven pm."

"Where did you get this data? Does the station provide it?"

"No, definitely not. It's out there. Most of it's free public records or on web pages from the state or counties. Financial transactions, vehicle registrations, criminal records, we get most of it from the Nexis database. It has everything. Just need to know what you're looking for and how it relates."

McBayne nodded, her mind still processing all the information.

Waters continued the demo of his state of the art data system. "Split checks makes it easy to connect people to the same place at the same time. We have several of those with these five couples in local restaurants and bars." He pointed to the transactions with different colored lines connecting them. "All are on Friday evenings over the last three months. Some before seven, some after ten. Also, social media, Facebook friends and location posts put people together. Then, of course, Google images can get you a picture of just about anyone, especially high profile people like these."

"How can you see private Facebook data?"

"Most people let anyone view their page, they don't understand the security settings. And if they do have it hidden, you become friends with them."

"You're Facebook friends with all these people?"

"Not me per se." He gave her a sly smile.

"Not you, then who?"

"I have a few Facebook aliases… an old woman, a teenage boy, girl in her twenties."

"Okay, now that's creepy."

"People like to have a lot of friends. I use their vanity against them. Did you just accept a friend request from Martha Graves, a distant great aunt?"

McBayne thought for a second. "Yes…how did you know that?"

"Because, I'm Martha Graves."

McBayne laughed. "Are you fucking kidding me? You're Martha Graves?"

He nodded. "I had to find out about my new partner. You didn't Google me when you found out we were partners?"

She nodded. "That's not the same thing….all right, continue, we'll talk about this later."

Waters returned to his high-tech demo. McBayne was still freaked out about how easily he tricked her into friending him, well, friending Martha. He clicked on the relationship line between Shaun Williams and Charles Browning. "Browning buys a new car from Williams' Audi dealership every two years." He clicked on the Williams and Spiers dashed line. "Emma Spiers and Sky Williams are on several charities together."

"This is unbelievable." McBayne started to realize the power of the data and this system.

"So, all this data and relationships, direct or inferred, reveals a definite pattern. Over the last several weeks, and mostly on Friday night roughly between seven to nine, this group of people seems to be meeting at the Spiers house."

"For what?" McBayne asked, fully expecting him to have that answer as well.

"I have no idea."

"Well, we need to find that out."

Waters nodded.

"Can I ask you something?" McBayne said. "What's that smell? It's very distracting."

"Oh, it's coffee."

"It smells fantastic."

"Do you want a cup?"

"Yes. I have a feeling we'll be up looking at this for a while too."

Waters stood and walked into the kitchen. McBayne followed then stopped on the living room side of the kitchen counter. She was still preoccupied with what she'd just seen and its implications.

She motioned toward the monitors. "Why is this here and not at the station?"

"No room, and the chief won't let me keep it there," Waters said as he reached for one of the mugs on the counter and poured coffee into it. "It gets in the way of *real* detective work," he said, in what appeared to be Chance Waters' version of sarcasm. "Cream okay?"

"Sure. Just a bit of sugar if you have it."

He poured some cream into her coffee mug and part of a packet of sugar, then slid the cup over to his partner. She picked it up, smelled it, and took a sip. "Holy shit, that's good. What is this?"

"It's Café Britt Organic from Costa Rica, Brunta region."

"Of course," she said sarcastically. "I need to get some of this."

"You have to brew it correctly, too," Waters added. "That's what makes the difference."

"What do you mean?"

"It's pretty easy. Just use distilled water, non-recycled filters, and use a Cuisinart coffee maker. They're the best."

"Right, that easy. Just like your little computer setup there."

She took another drink and a look of pure pleasure came over her face. "Christ, no wonder you can't drink coffee from fast food joints." She returned to the case. "Why don't you just print this out and show the chief?"

"It's still just circumstantial evidence, and mostly speculation right now."

"We need to start interviewing these people, especially in that inner circle."

"By the time we do that we'll be pulled off the case. If they were there that night, they're not going to admit it easily. And we only have until Tuesday to come up with something solid."

"Can the lab help?"

"Not without complete CSI, which they wouldn't do for this case. They would have to construct something from my photos to prove it was a blow to the head and not a fall."

"Dammit." She took another sip of her coffee. The case was quickly falling apart again, but at least she had discovered a new, delightful, warm beverage. "Well, have them do that. Send them your photos."

"They don't have the technology to process them, even if they wanted to."

She looked at her partner. He had his 'I have something to tell you' look. He wouldn't be very good at poker. "What?" she asked him.

"There is one possibility." He paused. "I have a friend, Calvin. He's kind of a forensics hobbyist. He's good, very smart. I use him on complex physical evidence and accident scenes like this."

"Well, let's get him over here."

"Can't. He lives in Louisiana, by my hometown."

"Shit." She took another sip of coffee. "Can I get some more of this?" Without waiting for an answer, she slid the cup across the counter toward him.

He looked at the cup, it wasn't even half empty yet. "I was thinking of driving out there tomorrow and meeting with him. He said he'd be available after two o'clock. He works nights, sleeps most of the day until after lunch."

"And when were you going to tell me this? Remember me, your partner?"

He handed back her coffee mug. "Umm, right now."

"Were you going to invite me?"

"Tomorrow's Saturday. It's our day off."

"I don't care."

"I thought you'd have plans."

"Plans, like what?"

"I don't know, going camping. Maybe doing some mushrooms with your girlfriends."

"Camping trip? Not this weekend. And no, I don't do drugs. I only tried it that one time. And I'm never doing it again after that experience."

"Well then, I guess you can come if you want. There's just one thing."

"What?"

"I have to stop at my mom's. I have a new computer for her."

"That's fine."

"And staying overnight. She'll be upset if I come out there and don't stay over."

"Cool, I'll pack a bag."

Waters looked at her. He seemed uncomfortable at the sudden change of events.

They went back to the computers and spent the next few hours reviewing all the data he had assembled on the five couples and even the next round of possible contacts. McBayne was overwhelmed by all the information and how it was connected, but it was obvious this group of five couples was meeting every Friday evening, and almost certainly were there the night Frank Thomas died.

They had new hope that they had caught a break in the case.

CHAPTER 19

It was noon on the dot when Detective Waters pulled into the rock driveway of the house where Detective McBayne lived. She rented the top floor. They were up late reviewing all the data Waters had gathered and tracing the relationships and financial transactions of the five couples. The noon departure allowed them to sleep in a little before the long drive to Shreveport.

Waters waited impatiently for a few minutes when a woman in a white sundress made her way down the wooden stairs on the side of the house. He could see the faint outline of her bra and panties in the sunlight behind her as she approached the car.

Her hair was down and covered part of her face. It was curlier than he would have imagined. She was showing more skin then he'd seen in their brief time together—her shoulders, legs and arms all exposed thanks to her outfit. She even sported some makeup.

She opened the back door and put her backpack on the seat. The seat behind Waters had a small gym bag, a computer case, and his leather briefcase.

"Good morning, Aunt Martha," she said and slid into the seat beside him.

"Good morning. You're late."

She looked at her watch. "Three minutes?"

"We'll have to make up the time on the highway."

She gave him a curious look. "Okay. Is that the computer for your mom?"

"Yes," he said, unsettled by either her appearance or her tardiness—maybe both. He was still looking down at her outfit.

"What?" she asked, obviously realizing he was distracted.

"Nothing...you look different."

"I'm meeting my boyfriend's best friend and his mother. I have to look nice."

"What?"

"It's a joke."

"Oh, right."

He pulled out of the driveway and they made their way east to the outer belt to pick up Route 30 toward Louisiana. Dallas, like all big cities, was almost unrecognizable on the weekend with the decrease in traffic. It looked deserted compared to the activity on a weekday, but made for a pleasant drive out of the city.

"I only had one cup of coffee this morning, so we don't have to stop and pee a bunch of times, okay?"

He looked over at her. "Good."

"What's that?" she asked and pointed to a new gadget connected to the dashboard just above his car stereo.

"It's a satellite radio receiver."

"Really. When did you get that?"

"I put it in this morning."

"You did all that this morning?"

"Yeah. It's not that hard."

"I guess. Turn it on. Let's check it out."

Waters reached down and hit the power button. It made a low beep and a small display area lit up.

"Let's see what Chance Waters has selected for stations," she said and started pressing the preset buttons. The first one was country, then classic rock, an oldies station, then the fourth one said 'The Eagle' in the little display area. She stopped. "An Eagles station?"

"Yes, I believe it is."

She looked at him. "Detective Waters, you installed satellite radio and have it preset to the Eagles just in time for our two hour trip to Shreveport? The detective in me would deduce you did that for me."

He became flustered and wasn't sure how to reply. "Well, its two and half hours to Shreveport."

"Oh, okay," she said.

He continued to look straight ahead.

She hit the other two presets, news and talk radio, then quickly moved on. Then she started browsing the other stations, stopping when she got to the country music section of the dial. "Holy cow, here's one that plays all rodeo songs."

Waters looked over at her. "Really?"

"No," she said and started to laugh. She continued to laugh harder after seeing the disappointed look on his face. "I'm sorry, that was mean. Let's just stick with 'The Eagle' for now."

She was still smiling and didn't look sorry.

They drove for a while listening to a few of the less recognizable Eagles songs, then "Take It to the Limit" came on.

"Oh! Great song. This one was sung by Randy Meisner, not Glenn Frey or Don Henley. Randy had a higher voice and could get to the high notes."

Waters nodded.

"As the band became more successful, Randy didn't like the spotlight and became more insecure about his ability to hit the high notes. He started refusing to sing the song live. Glenn got really pissed, can't blame him, that's what the fans wanted to hear. Then they got into a fight after one show. After the tour ended, Randy quit the band. That's when they replaced him with Timothy B. Schmit."

"Oh," Waters replied.

They continued to drive listening to Randy Meisner hit the high notes. McBayne sang along, but not so loud that it was annoying. The song ended and the station started talking about another possible Eagles reunion tour. McBayne turned the volume down and looked at him. "So, what's your mom like?"

"She's okay, thinks she's funnier than she is. Likes to give me advice. If she likes you she'll make you a quilt."

"I'm getting a quilt?"

"If she likes you."

"Oh, she'll like me. Is your dad still around?" she asked.

"No."

"Divorced?"

"Umm, no."

She continued to look at him, silently. He noticed she does that when she wants an answer but doesn't want to be pushy.

"He died in a car accident when I was a kid."

"I'm sorry."

They continued to head East—Waters driving exactly the speed limit, not one mile above or below, and obeying every driving rule. More Eagles songs came on mixed with Henley, Frey, and Walsh recordings from their solo careers. Detective McBayne apparently didn't care for these. They were cheating on the band according to her, even though some of them were "Good songs, mind you".

McBayne was a worthy passenger, she was good at eliminating the awkward silent moments that he had with most people. She said pretty much whatever popped into her head. As she was talking, he couldn't help but notice the top of her dress. At that angle he could see her bra and the top of her breasts pushing up out of it. The bottom of her dress was riding up over her thighs too showing her legs. It was distracting him as a driver, and he didn't like being distracted. At least he always thought he didn't.

She continued recounting Eagles trivia. Waters continued to feign interest. Eventually, she changed the subject. "So, yoga. What's that all about?"

"It's my main workout. I run a little, too."

"Yeah, you look like a runner. I tried yoga once. Didn't care for it. Too much time in the same place. I thought my wrists were going to snap in two on that damn upward dog and downward dog."

"You get used to that. You have to stick with it for three or four times. It's as much mental as physical."

"You're right about that. And I don't like the mental part. I'd rather kick something."

"You do kickboxing?" he asked.

"Yes, and a lot of self-defense workouts."

"Really?"

"You have to when you're five seven and a hundred and twenty-eight pounds."

"You ever get into a fight when you were patrolling the street?"

"One time a perp, good sized dude, took a swing at me while I was trying to cuff him."

"And?"

"I punched him in the solar plexus, he went down. That's what I learned in self-defense. If they're bigger and stronger than you, go for the solar plexus. A lot of people say kick them in the groin, but they're expecting that, and it's a harder target. Everyone puts their hands up to protect their face, that leaves their plexus wide open."

"Really?"

"Yes, especially vain bastards. They don't want to get hit in the face, break a nose, or lose a tooth. Hit them right here."

She reached over and touched his stomach just under his chest. "There, feel that?" He nodded. "They can't breathe, a good kick in the face, fight over."

Waters reached down and felt his stomach where she touched him. He's going to have to research Solar Plexus.

"Great song!" McBayne said and turned the volume up as the beginning guitar chords to 'Peaceful Easy Feeling' began to play.

"This might be my all-time favorite Eagles song. I switch between it and 'Best of My Love.' But then there's 'Take It Easy', too."

"The song that started it all," Waters chimed in.

She looked at him, a bit stunned. "Did you know that's what Glenn Frey says at concerts when they play it?"

Waters shrugged.

They drove a while longer and the song finished.

"So, how did you meet Calvin?" she asked.

"I met him online when I was taking college courses during high school. We were both taking a computer security class. He could have taught it, he already knew more than the professor. I moved to Dallas when I got my first job as a patrolman, but we stayed in touch. He tests new games and simulators now. I use him for forensics when our lab can't get to it or doesn't have the equipment."

"And the chief pays for that?"

"Oh no, Calvin and I barter. He'll do forensics for me and I'll help him with software or get him some data that he can't get."

They continued the drive, talking intermittently, all the while listening to the Eagles station. Finally, they left the State of Texas. Shreveport was right over the state line.

CHAPTER 20

Detective McBayne was now thoroughly lost as her partner began traversing a maze of smaller country roads. She couldn't find her way back to the highway if her life depended on it. They passed under an old rock bridge with train tracks running along the top. The opening was barely wide enough to fit two cars passing through at the same time.

In front of them was a classic Southern American small town, complete with a large white church and a common area just off of Main Street. The people of the town were going about their normal Saturday afternoon business, just like their ancestors probably had for generations.

Waters followed Main Street to the far end of town, which took less than a minute going fifteen miles an hour and stopping at both stop lights. He pulled into the parking lot of an old general store. The sign said Chauncey's Market. Most places like this one had long since been replaced by quickie marts with gas pumps or swallowed up by huge retail chain stores.

Waters got out of the car and grabbed his brown leather briefcase from the back seat, locked the car and headed into the store. She followed.

This might have been the last place Detective McBayne expected to meet one of Water's friends. Then again, she'd never met one of his friends. "We're meeting him at a general store?" she asked and looked around like she was missing something.

"It's a front."

"What?"

"You'll see. Calvin's upstairs." He pointed to the second floor of the building. "Do you want something to drink?"

"Sure. A water would be good."

Waters went to the beverage cooler and grabbed a bottle of water, a dark red Vitamin drink, and a chocolate milk. She assumed the Vitamin water was for him, he did eat and drink fairly healthy, except for chocolate milkshakes. He paid the young, pleasant-looking girl working the register. McBayne got the feeling they knew each other but it was hard to tell with Chance Waters. Even encounters with people he knew could be awkward. He grabbed the bag of drinks and they headed to the back of the store.

A long hallway lead outside. There was a bathroom door on the right.

"Can I stop in here for a second?" McBayne asked.

"Sure." He waited outside until his partner returned.

He opened the back door of the store. Behind the building was a thickly wooded area. She still had no clue where they were headed. Waters turned right and walked toward an old wooden staircase that lead to the second floor.

The boards creaked under their footsteps as they climbed the stairs. The entire structure looked like it was built more as an afterthought, and definitely not by a professional. McBayne squinted trying to peer through the upstairs windows. They were covered with something dark on the inside, or possibly painted over. She looked at the end of the building, there was a set of three large satellite dish receivers mounted on the roof, definitely not normal satellite TV issue.

They reached the landing at the top of the stairs. Waters handed the bag of drinks to McBayne and approached the door. He knocked. No answer. Knocked again, louder this time. They waited, still no answer. He knocked once more—nothing.

Waters put his briefcase down on the deck. He leaned over the wooden railing on the left, reached out as far as he could, and knocked on the window. A loud crack echoed through the woods as the railing snapped in two. He began to fall over the side. At the last second, he reached out and braced himself against the far side of the window. He looked like a gymnast doing half an iron cross.

McBayne, caught completely off guard, dropped the bag of drinks, grabbed his free arm and pulled him back onto the porch.

He composed himself. "Thanks."

"Holy shit," she said looking at him. "You're stronger than you look."

The door opened. Standing in front of them was a short, stocky man of about thirty-five with long sandy colored hair. He was wearing Bermuda shorts, flip-flops, and a t-shirt with some formula on it that a scientist trying to be hip would wear. He was unshaven and generally disheveled.

Calvin, squinting his eyes, seemed to be having trouble adjusting to the morning light; well, morning for him. A smile appeared on his face when he realized it was his old buddy, Chance Waters. He looked over at the broken railing. "Dude, you're breaking my stuff?"

Calvin noticed Detective McBayne standing behind Waters and immediately cocked his head and did a full body scan of her. He looked at Waters. "She's with you?"

"This is Detective McBayne, my partner."

He walked past Waters and continued staring.

"Why, hello, my dear, Calvin Bartholomew at your service."

"Nice to meet you, Mr. Bartholomew." She put her hand out to shake.

He took her hand, raised it to his mouth, and kissed the back of it; looking her in the eyes the entire time.

She tried desperately not to break out laughing. "Thanks for helping us with the case."

"It's my pleasure, darling. Please, call me Cal." He looked at Detective Waters, "You still call me Calvin though." Back to Detective McBayne. "And what's your real name? I'm not calling you detective."

"It's Carlie."

"Very well, Carlie. Please come in."

The detectives picked up their stuff on the landing and followed Calvin into the apartment.

"Chance, you didn't say you were bringing this beautiful creature. I would have cleaned up the place, and myself." He looked at her. "I'm usually much more handsome. Been up all night helping our government keep the bad guys out."

"Is that true?" She looked at Waters for confirmation.

He shrugged.

It was dark inside Calvin's apartment, similar to Waters' place. It consisted mainly of one large room with a kitchen sink and refrigerator at one end. Two doors at the opposite end likely lead to the bathroom and a bedroom.

The center of the room looked like the control panel of a spaceship. Three modern looking computer tables contained different sizes and styles of computers and monitors. The high-tech equipment made an interesting contrast in an old apartment on top of a 1950's general store. Other machines stacked on crates below the tables looked like scanners and oversized printers.

"The bathroom's over there if anyone needs to use it." Calvin pointed to a door on the opposite wall.

"I should go before we get started," Detective Waters said. He dropped his leather case off by the chairs on his way.

Calvin walked to the middle of the room in front of the computers. McBayne followed.

"Have a seat, my dear," he said and held the back of her chair.

He placed another chair on the opposite side of his, presumably for Detective Waters.

McBayne removed the drinks from the bag and put the water at her feet. She presented the other two to Calvin. He selected the chocolate milk, opened it, and took a big swig. "Ah, breakfast of champions."

She put the vitamin water on the table in front of the empty chair reserved for her partner.

"Are you two partners, or *partners*?" Calvin asked and made a circle with his thumb and finger on one hand and stuck the index finger of his other hand in the hole a couple times, making the international signal for two people screwing.

McBayne laughed. "No." It would probably have been insulting coming from anyone else, or about anyone else besides Detective Waters.

"Oh, good then." He smiled.

"So, you live here?" she asked, mostly to change the subject.

"Yes, live and work."

Calvin started typing on his keyboard, shutting down some programs and starting others. Waters returned from the bathroom and sat in the empty chair, reached into his briefcase, pulled out a small flash drive, and handed it to his friend.

Calvin plugged it into the USB port on the computer at his feet. A window popped up on the main monitor and displayed several images. He clicked on the first picture and it opened in the center of the screen. It was one of Waters' photos of the accident scene taken from ground level. The balcony was in the background with Frank Thomas lying dead on the floor face up. The doors to the balcony were on the left. The overturned table was farther back behind the body.

Just like with Waters, Calvin's persona changed when he was using his computer. He was no longer a comical Don Juan.

"So, you want to know if this guy fell or was clobbered?"

"Yes," Waters answered.

"Head injury is on the side, so of course we suspect a blow, not a fall," McBayne commented.

Calvin looked at the lady detective and raised his eyebrows. "Pretty and smart. I like that." He winked at her.

He clicked on an icon and another program started. It looked complex, had several menus, buttons, and different sections of what looked to be drawing tools. It had a lot more scientific looking options than Photoshop or other popular image editing software.

Calvin dragged the picture from the other window onto the program. It became embedded in the middle and dotted grid lines appeared on the photo. All the objects in the picture became outlined and raised as if they were separate entities.

"So, this program automatically identifies all objects in the frame. Kind of like how Facebook identifies people's faces in a photo and you can tag them." He looked at the two detectives. They nodded. "It tries to figure out, or make an educated guess, what's in the room."

He clicked the mouse on the outline that had formed around Frank Thomas's body. Text appeared below it that said "Human" and had two circles to select, "Yes" or "No." He checked "Yes." Another series of questions popped up. Sex was already selected as male.

"How does it know he's a male?" Detective McBayne asked.

Calvin shook the mouse over Franks groin area and looked at the lady detective. "From the bulge here." He then moved it over to Franks' chest, "and no bulges here." Then he winked at her. "Didn't you take health in high school, Carlie?"

She laughed. "Yes, got an A in it too."

"I bet you did," Calvin said in as sexy a voice as a computer nerd in Bermuda shorts can muster.

He continued with the data entry. "Height and weight of the victim?"

"Six two, one eighty-three," Waters replied.

"A big one." Calvin typed in the data.

"How did you know that?" McBayne asked her partner.

"Driver's license, but everyone lies on those, so I used his latest medical records."

"We're assuming he was standing here?" Calvin asked and clicked on the floor by Thomas's feet.

Waters nodded.

He moved the pointer onto Thomas's head, pressed it, and dragged him up to the standing position. The program made the deceased man bend at the knees and waist like a live person would. It was like watching a dead man come to life.

Next, Calvin selected the wine table. A confirmation box appeared that said, "Furniture: Table" and a different set of questions popped up.

Waters answered them in succession for weight, top, legs.

"Four foot, granite, cast iron."

Calvin stopped, grabbed his chocolate milk and finished it. He tossed the empty container toward the trash can fifteen feet away. It went in. He looked at McBayne and smiled.

"Nice shot. Athletic and smart, I like that," she said.

Calvin looked at Waters and nodded like he was making progress with the female detective. Next, he highlighted the box containing the weight of the table.

"Twenty-three pounds," Waters informed him.

"If someone hit him with that, it must have been a man," Calvin commented.

"Or a strong woman," McBayne said defending her gender.

"Of course," he said and dragged the table so it was standing about six feet from where Thomas was now upright in the picture. "So, your suspect says he just fell onto the table?"

"Yes," Waters answered. "He said he wasn't in the room at the time, so he doesn't know how it really happened."

Calvin drew a line with an arrow from the side of Thomas's head where the injury was to the edge of the table, where he would have hit his head.

"What's this program?" McBayne asked.

"It's high-end animation software, beta version. Not for commercial use yet. It's used for gaming mostly, but works great for recreating crime scenes."

"We can't use it in court to get a conviction," Waters added. "Sometimes it's just good to produce clues, or see if people are lying."

Calvin pointed the mouse to the bottom of the legs on the table. "These are rubber?"

"Yes."

"Floor surface type?"

"Spanish tile, high slip resistance, probably around R-twelve."

"Tacky. The table shouldn't slide that much. Definitely not where it ended up."

"That's what I was thinking," Waters confirmed.

McBayne watched the two scientists go back and forth like she was watching a tennis match. Again, Calvin typed the data into the information area for the floor surface.

"Ready? Let's play," he said and hit the green go button.

The program started. In slow motion, it showed Thomas falling. His body turned so the side of his head would hit the corner of the table. His head made contact and blood immediately squirted out of the wound. The table slid across the floor about a foot. It teetered a couple times, then fell over. Thomas' body ended up on the floor face down.

"Interesting," Waters said.

"What?" McBayne asked.

Calvin picked up a pen and pointed to the table on the screen.

"Because of the high viscosity between the table and floor, and the weight of the table, it would only slide this far." He pointed to the table on the screen.

"Dead guy would have landed face down, not face up like they found him." He looked at Waters. "Right?"

Waters nodded.

Calvin continued. "But from the original picture, the table was found way back here behind dead guy, maybe eight feet away. And he was face-up. They didn't touch anything or move him did they?"

"Said they didn't," Waters answered and looked at McBayne.

"Yes. I asked a couple times. They said no one moved anything. There was blood on both of the women after the accident, though."

"So, this is where the table should have ended up. Now, let's simulate how the fall would have had to have happened for the table to end up where it did. Watch this."

Calvin hit a button and it reset Thomas and the table to their original positions. He drew a line with an arrow from the upright table to the spot it ended up from the crime scene picture. Then he hit the go button. "And action."

The animation showed Thomas stepping to his left, then falling backward toward the table. It looked like he was diving into it. The table went flying end over end to the spot it ended up in the original picture. Thomas's body hit face first, then flipped over onto his back.

"Very unlikely," Waters concluded.

"Physically impossible, I think," Calvin added. "He would have had to dive into it, like a football player making a tackle."

The three spent half an hour changing values, rerunning animations, trying to come up with different scenarios. All were contrived, none resulted in an outcome where the table ended up where it was in the accident scene photos.

Calvin summarized the demonstrations to the group. "Each scenario gets assigned a rating of likelihood. None are in the accepted range of probability. I think something else happened to your dead guy."

"Well, I think that about does it," Waters said and stood. "What do you think, detective?"

"I agree. I think we're done here."

"Calvin, can you do a time lapse print out of both scenarios? We need to show the chief this. Maybe it'll buy us some more time."

"Sure." Calvin hit a few buttons on his screen and one of the printers beside them started up.

Detective Waters took the printouts and put them in his briefcase. They grabbed their gear and made their way toward the door.

"You're heading out. Don't you want to stay for dinner? I make a hell of a meatloaf," Calvin offered.

"Sorry, have to get to Mom's," Waters informed him.

McBayne shrugged like she had to go too.

"You can stay. You don't want to go to his old house, do you? Boring."

"He's my ride." She reached out her hand to shake.

Calvin ignored it and gave her a big hug. He continued the hug long enough for it to become uncomfortable.

"Thanks for your help, Cal. That was interesting," she said, trying to pull back out of his grasp.

Calvin released her and looked at Waters. "Is she serious?"

"I'm not sure a lot of the time."

"Yes, I'm serious. This is neat stuff. Maybe you can teach me it someday."

Calvin moved closer to her, took both of her hands in his, and said in a soft, sexy voice, "I would love that."

McBayne smiled as he released her hands. Waters shook his old friend's hand and they headed out the door, avoiding the broken railing on the way out. Calvin followed and watched them leave from the top of the stairs, his eyes on Carlie the entire way.

The detectives left through the general store, made their way to the parking lot, and got into their car. They pulled out onto the road and began the twenty minute trip to the Waters' residence.

Detective Waters spoke without looking at McBayne, "I think Calvin likes you."

She turned and looked at him, surprised he would even notice something like that. "He's not really my type."

CHAPTER 21

The blue Ford with Texas plates made its way to the end of a long, overgrown country road. It turned, then followed a narrow driveway to the front of the Waters' home. Before them was a picturesque two-story country house with a large front porch containing two rocking chairs. The view from the road invited people to sit and have a glass of lemonade.

The house was nestled in the middle of several perfectly placed Oak trees with Spanish moss hanging from the branches. The huge trees appeared to be protecting the house and its occupants from the elements. The lawn was outlined with freshly maintained flower beds and an occasional bird bath.

Detective McBayne looked over at her partner and smiled. "Adorable."

Two worn tire tracks with a grass path growing between them lead to the side of the house to an old garage with doors that opened like a barn. Waters stopped the car in front of the garage and grabbed their bags from the backseat. They made their way to the front of the house and onto the porch. He opened the front screen door. "Mom, we're here."

A short, jolly looking woman wearing an apron came out of the kitchen door into the hallway. She gave her son a big hug. "My boy is home." He hugged her back, a little self-conscious. They separated and Mrs. Waters spotted her son's partner.

"And you must be Ms. McBayne."

"Carlie, please."

Mrs. Waters gave her a big hug too.

The unmistakable smell of freshly baked chocolate chip cookies was in the air.

"Nice to meet you, Mrs. Waters."

"Please, dear, call me Evelyn."

"Okay, Evelyn."

"How was the drive? Did you meet with your friend?"

Waters nodded.

Evelyn stood back to get a better look at her boy. "Chance, you're going to be in the sitting room, and I'm putting Ms. McBayne, I mean Carlie, in your old room."

"Oh, I can't take Detective Waters' bedroom."

"Nonsense. It has the most comfortable bed in the house and you're a guest. And we go by first names in this house, so no more detective this and that."

McBayne smiled. "Okay then."

They walked into the sitting room. Waters put his bag on the couch.

"Is that my new computer?" Evelyn asked her son.

"Sure is. I'll set it up later."

"You're a good boy." She kissed him on the cheek.

They turned and headed back into the hallway. Evelyn led them up a narrow staircase with creaky small steps that would never pass inspection today.

"Up here is Chance's old room."

The detectives followed her. Waters started to feel uneasy, he rarely had someone in his room, even as a kid.

They entered the room and might as well have gone back twenty-five years in time. It was the bedroom of a little boy with a small twin bed and an old wooden desk and chair. All the pictures were of Waters as a child, most of them with his Dad fishing, sitting on the tractor, and playing catch with a football. There were trophies on a bookshelf but it wasn't apparent what they were for. They weren't the classic sports trophies most boys have.

McBayne looked around the room, she seemed quite entertained, looking at a picture then over to her partner. On the wall above the bed was a poster of Albert Einstein with his tongue sticking out playfully and a quote underneath that said, "The difference between stupidity and genius is that genius has its limits."

"Cool," MacBayne said and pointed to it. She read the quote out loud and laughed, then walked over to the trophies. "What are these for?"

"Oh, that was for the spelling bee," Evelyn answered proudly.

"Chance was the district champion. Then he got to the States and an Indian girl kicked his ass. Didn't she?" She looked at her son. He wasn't happy.

"Metamorphosis," Waters mumbled to himself.

McBayne looked at him.

"That's the word the Indian girl beat him on," Evelyn informed her.

"Yes, that should be in a spelling bee," he said sarcastically.

"Wow, the competitive side of Chance Waters," McBayne replied.

At the end of the bed was a bookshelf with old science books and a stack of puzzle magazines. On the top shelf was a large school picture of Waters wearing a checkered shirt with an odd grin on his face. McBayne walked over to it. "Oh my God, when was this taken?"

"Third grade," Evelyn said.

"You were so cute. What's that smirk for? I've never seen that look."

Waters blushed. "Two girls were trying to get me to smile."

"Well, it almost worked," she said and continued looking at the picture, then at Detective Waters, almost like she was trying to reconcile the two images.

"You can leave your bag up here, sweetie," Waters' mom informed her.

Evelyn continued the upstairs tour, showing McBayne the bathroom and the other bedrooms. One was Evelyn's, the other was filled with storage boxes. The ceiling was so low it felt like they were going to hit their heads. Everything in the house was old, probably original, but still in good shape. They made their way back downstairs into the kitchen.

They spent the afternoon having cookies, talking, and getting acquainted. Evelyn's living room walls were lined with quilts she had made. McBayne made a point of letting her know how much she liked them.

Detective McBayne spent part of the afternoon up in her room resting while Waters checked the house, making sure everything was in working order. They took a walk through the wooded trail behind the house and down to a beautiful old pond where Waters use to fish with his Dad. Eventually, they returned to the house for dinner.

Already Gone

***

"That smells wonderful, Evelyn," McBayne said as she entered the kitchen.

"Get cleaned up, dinner's about ready."

They enjoyed a classic country meal—roasted pork loin, mashed potatoes with gravy, fresh green beans with bacon chunks, and warm dinner rolls. Real butter in everything, nothing gluten free or low cal.

Waters helped his mom do the dishes. McBayne tried to pitch in, but Evelyn wouldn't allow it. She cleared her dishes from the table, then went out onto the porch to watch the setting sun.

Several minutes passed and the front door opened. Evelyn came out of the house carrying two coffee mugs. "Would you like a drink, dear?"

"Yes, thank you."

Evelyn handed her the mug. "Chance is setting up my computer, so we can sit and visit for a spell."

McBayne looked down into the coffee cup, not sure what was in it. She smelled it, then took a drink. It surprised her. "That's not coffee."

"No, it's apple wine. We make our own in this area. Oh no, you're not a recovering alcoholic, are you?"

"No, I'm not." McBayne laughed at the blunt question, then took another drink. "This is good. Everything you make is delicious, Evelyn."

"Thank you, that's so sweet. Don't tell Chance we're out here getting snookered. He's a teetotaler you know."

"Yes, I was starting to get that feeling."

The ladies looked out over the peaceful yard. The setting sun was still making its way between the trees, creating long shadows of anything that got in its way. The bugs were buzzing around the remaining light, distracting them from the humans on the porch. They could feel the coolness of the approaching night trying to displace the heat from the day.

"Are you married, dear?"

"No, ma'am. Came close one time."

"How old are you?"

"Twenty-seven; will be twenty-eight next month."

"Plenty of time. Women are having kids until they're forty these days. Of course, you don't want to be a fifty-year-old first-time mother."

McBayne took another sip of her wine. "Chance said his dad passed away when he was young?"

"Yes, in a car crash. Drunk driver, t-boned them at an intersection way out on Route 169."

"Them?"

"Oh yes, Chance was in the car. They were coming back from the stock car races down in Sabine. It was late at night. That always worried me," she said and took a drink of her wine.

"Oh my God, I didn't know that."

"The drunk driver and Ralph, my husband, were killed instantly. Ralph's truck rolled over on its roof. Chance was trapped in there for almost an hour until someone finally came by."

"I'm sorry, Evelyn. That's horrible."

"When they found him he was covered in blood. They thought it was his, but it wasn't, was his Dad's. Chance didn't have a scratch on him."

McBayne looked at Evelyn. She had a sad look on her face like she hadn't thought of that story in a while. She took another drink, paused, then continued. "He was never the same after that. Didn't speak a word for two months. Must have been in shock still. He used to be the happiest little kid until then. Loved his dad. They did everything together; fishing, working on cars, going to the rodeo over the border in Texas."

Evelyn took another sip of wine while looking out over the yard.

"He started to come out of it a little in high school, made a couple friends. Then one night he went to a party with his school mates. I knew he was excited because he wore his dress jeans and Sunday school shirt."

McBayne smiled. "I bet he was adorable."

"Something happened that night. He came home early, upset. Wouldn't come out of his room for days."

"What happened?"

"I don't know, he never talked about it. Wouldn't even go back to school. Had to finish out taking online courses and classes at the college. Aced his GED so that wasn't a problem, but no colleges would give him a scholarship without a diploma."

"Did you ever find out what happened?"

"No, I asked around but never found out. He was always a pretty sensitive kid. Was probably just normal bullying he didn't know how to handle. Kids can be mean sometimes."

"That they can."

The ladies finished their drinks and had another. They continued to talk about how McBayne became a cop and then a detective and more stories about Waters as a kid. Eventually, Detective McBayne excused herself and went upstairs to take a shower and get ready for bed.

***

It was almost ten o'clock at night. Waters and his mom sat at the kitchen table talking. He had a mug in front of him.

Detective McBayne came down the stairs into the kitchen. He watched her walk by and smile at him. She had on a navy blue Chicago Bears night shirt with the number fifty-four on the front. That was another first, a woman in pajamas in Waters' kitchen.

"Is that hot chocolate?" she asked.

He nodded.

"How sweet, having a cup of cocoa with your mommy." He was pretty sure she was making fun of him. "I should take a picture and show it around the squad room." And that confirmed it.

"Evelyn, okay if I get a glass of water to take upstairs?"

"Of course, dear." She said and started to get up.

"Stay right where you are, I'll get it. You've done enough today."

"The glasses are right there," Evelyn said and pointed to the tall cabinet beside the refrigerator.

McBayne moved in front of the cabinet and opened it. The glass she wanted was on the top shelf. She got onto her tip-toes so she could reach it. As she did, her night shirt rose up and exposed her underwear. She was wearing red, tight-fitting, women's jockey style shorts. They complimented her bottom quite well.

Evelyn nudged her son and made a motion toward the woman in their kitchen. He mouthed the word *stop* to her and attempted to turn his head. He wasn't successful.

His partner filled the glass with water from the sink and turned to her hosts at the table. "What time are we heading out tomorrow, Detective? I mean, Chance."

He was still looking down at her shapely legs.

"Chance?"

He looked up. "Oh, umm, right after breakfast I was thinking."

"Sounds good." She looked at Mrs. Waters. "Evelyn, thank you for everything."

"You're welcome. I love having my boy home, especially when he brings a girl."

"Oh, he does this a lot, does he?"

"No, this is the first time," Waters corrected her.

"Really?" she said like she was surprised. He didn't catch the sarcasm.

McBayne started to walk past them, then stopped by the table and looked down at her partner. "This was a lot of fun today." She gave him a kiss on the cheek, turned, and went up the stairs to her room.

He looked at his Mom, she had a huge smile on her face. He gave her the 'stop it' look. They continued their talk, he made sure she knew everything there was to know about her new computer. It was the first laptop she'd had.

He finished his hot chocolate, kissed his mom goodnight, and they both retired to their rooms.

***

Detective McBayne was lying in bed. She finished reading her email on her phone and checked her social media sites. She never posted items for herself but liked reading what her family and friends in Chicago were up to. She also unfriended Martha Graves.

She leaned up on the bed and lifted the old wooden window pane so it opened about a foot. A fresh breeze rushed into the room. She snuggled down in the bed which was very comfortable—Evelyn was right about that. It was one of those mattresses that engulfs its occupant.

She pulled the freshly washed sheet and another homemade quilt over her body. She snuggled down in the bed, this was a comfortable house. As awkward as Chance Waters could make a person feel, his mother was the opposite. She quickly drifted off to sleep with the country breeze gently flowing over her face.

***

Detective Waters laid on the couch between a bed sheet and, of course, another one of his mother's quilts. He thought he knew every creak and sound in the old house, but sleeping downstairs he had discovered some new ones.

He thought about the Thomas case, were there any clues he was missing? He tried to put himself in the chief's position and figure out what he needed to hear to let them continue. It was obvious to him the story told by Spiers and the two women was not what happened. There were more pieces to this puzzle, he just had to find them. He needed more time, he wasn't going to let this puzzle go unfinished. Even if the chief pulled them off it, he would continue until all paths were exhausted.

His thoughts kept getting interrupted by the image of his partner on her tip toes, those shapely legs, and how sexy she made cotton jockey shorts look. He forced those thoughts out of his head and finally drifted off to sleep.

***

Sounds from the woods around the old country house continued to fill the night air. Crickets, raccoons, squirrels, and tree branches bending in the wind blended together and created a single chorus. A rainstorm threatened from the Gulf, but it wouldn't reach them with any precipitation.

The faint sound of footsteps making their way upstairs broke the silence inside the house. The door to Waters' childhood bedroom slowly opened. The moonlight coming in through the window provided some light to the room. A thin man wearing silk boxer shorts and a matching robe entered the room and shut the door behind him.

Chance Waters made his way over to the bed, knelt beside it, and looked at his sleeping partner. He cleared his throat to get her attention. She opened her eyes slowly, startled but not scared.

"Chance," she said in a low, sleepy voice.

Before she could say anything else he leaned in and kissed her. Soft and gentle.

She pulled away and looked at him. "What are you doing?" she said in a sleepy voice.

"Shhhh, we both knew this was going to happen."

"We can't do this," she said, "we're partners, it's against station policy."

"To hell with station policy." He let his robe fall to the ground behind him. His thin but toned body glimmered in the moonlight.

She reached up and placed the palms of her hands on his chest, moved them to his shoulders, then down his arms to his triceps. "Where did these come from?" she said as if he was hiding them from her the last couple of months.

In a smooth, sexy voice he said, "Yoga body."

She lifted the corner of the bedspread, he slid into the bed beside her. Their bodies now sharing the warmth of the thick blanket and welcoming mattress, protecting them from the cool, Louisiana night. They continued to kiss, slow and sensual like they were savoring every one. Occasionally they opened their eyes and looked at each other like it was the first time they'd seen one another.

His lips worked their way from her mouth, down her chin to her neck, gently kissing along the way. His warm breath tickled her ear. She shuddered. He continued down her neck to the top of her chest. His chin pushed the collar of her shirt down exposing the top of her breasts.

He stopped, looked up at her, then reached down and pulled her nightgown above her waist. It passed over her trim, kickboxer stomach, then over her chest, exposing her naked breasts. She blushed and arched her back, helping him remove it completely.

She could feel the coolness on her already rigid, sensitive nipples. He held her tightly, their chests pressed together. He slid down and she felt his mouth on one breast and his hand firmly cupping the other. Her heart pounded as he kissed and squeezed her sensitive nipples.

He looked up at her and whispered in that innocent, Cajun voice, "Is this okay?"

"Yes," she said in more of a moan.

His knee slowly worked its way between her legs, separating them. She trembled as his thigh pressed against her sensitive areas. He slid his mouth from her breasts down to her stomach, kissing and nuzzling along the way, hitting just the right places at the right time like she was controlling him with her mind. His chin pushed her panties down, the elastic trying to resist, but like her, it wasn't very effective. His face was getting dangerously close to between her legs. She started moaning deeper now.

His mouth made its way over her shorts, past her mound to her inner thigh. He started kissing his way back up, teasing her with his tongue as it playfully made its way under her jockey shorts.

She took a deep breath, her head tilted back and her eyes closed. He reached up with both hands and pulled her underwear down, over her long legs and her feet. He looked up at her and grinned, then his face disappeared between her legs. She couldn't take it anymore and let out a loud moan and then.

Detective McBayne's eyes flew open and she bolted up in bed. Her heart was racing and she struggled to catch her breath. For a few seconds, she couldn't remember where she was. Gradually it came to her, she was in Detective Waters childhood bedroom.

"Oh shit."

She looked straight ahead. The light from the window was centered on the grade school picture of Detective Waters. His face, with that peculiar smirk, staring directly at her—the childhood grin of his taking on a whole new meaning.

She looked around the room trying to regain her senses, reassuring herself that it really was just a dream. "Crap," she said, shook her head, and curled back into the bed and fell asleep.

***

The bright light shone through the window awakening Detective McBayne, for good this time. She crawled out of bed and walked down the hallway to the bathroom, her bare feet feeling the warn old wooden floor boards. She could hear the Waters talking downstairs as another delicious aroma rose from Evelyn's kitchen.

She got dressed, packed her bag, took the sheets off the bed, and made her way downstairs.

"Good morning, Carlie. Coffee?" Evelyn greeted her as she entered the kitchen.

"Yes, please. I'd love some," she said and put her bag down and sat at the table.

Evelyn put a mug in front of her, then filled it with coffee from an old percolator style coffee maker that heats up on the stove. Detective McBayne poured some cream from a mini pitcher into her cup, stirred in some sugar with a spoon, and took a sip. Very good, not quite as good as her son's, but in the ballpark. "Where's Chance?"

"He's outside checking the oil in his car. He should be in shortly."

"What was in that wine? I had the craziest dream last night."

"Really, what about?"

Carlie paused. "Oh, nothing, I don't really remember now."

They heard the front screen door open. A few seconds later Waters entered the kitchen. McBayne stared at him. She even blushed a little.

"Morning," he said.

"Morning to you."

He washed his hands in the kitchen sink and sat at the table beside her. She was still looking at him oddly. He finally noticed. "What?"

"Nothing." She leaned in and spoke softly. "Did you come into my room last night?"

"No." A thoroughly confused look on his face now.

Evelyn brought over two plates containing scrambled eggs with peppers, onions, and cheese, homemade biscuits cut open, and thick sausage gravy on top.

"Eat up. You folks have a long trip ahead of you."

McBayne took a bite of the biscuits and gravy. "Holy shit! That's better than Bob Evans." She put her hand over her mouth. "Oh, I'm sorry. I couldn't help myself."

"She curses a lot," Waters informed his mother while sampling the biscuits and gravy himself.

She looked at him. "Really, Waters? You're telling your mom on me?"

He shrugged. "You do swear a lot."

"These are fantastic, Evelyn. Are you trying to get me to stay here?"

"You're always welcome," she said and sat down at the table with a small plate for herself.

Typical small town breakfast table talk ensued. Evelyn updated her son on the latest happenings of the Water's friends and relatives. One Uncle recently spent the night in jail for being drunk and disorderly. A girl cousin broke up with her longtime boyfriend. And a close family friend took over the pizza place in town.

They finished their breakfast and everyone pitched in to clear the table. Waters retrieved his and Detective McBayne's bag from the living room and headed outside to the porch. He hugged his mom goodbye, gave her a kiss on the cheek, and went to the car.

McBayne walked out the front door of the house. Evelyn followed and handed her a basket with a plastic container and paper towel with something wrapped inside. It was still warm.

"What's this?"

"Some biscuits and gravy for you to take home."

"Oh, thank you, Evelyn. You've been so kind."

"Listen, dear." Evelyn paused, she looked like she was having trouble finding the right words. "I realize my son is…a bit odd. He's broken and I'm not sure he can ever be fixed. But something in him has changed. I can see it in his eyes and hear it in his voice."

"What is it?"

"I'm not sure, but I think I know who's responsible."

"Who?"

Evelyn cocked her head and smiled at Detective McBayne, gave her a long stare, then a big goodbye hug. She waved to her son and headed back into the house.

The female detective, still a bit dazed, got into the car. Waters turned the car around and they headed back down the old country road.

She looked at him. "This was a fun weekend, thanks for bringing me."

"More fun than camping?"

She grinned and nodded.

CHAPTER 22

The chief held up an oversized sheet of paper containing a series of images. He touched his chin with his thumb and index finger as his eyes darted from picture to picture. "So, there's no way it happened the way they said. That table couldn't have ended up where it was in your photos?"

McBayne and Waters, sitting in the chairs in front of the chief's desk, nodded.

"It's all theory and animation, but the science doesn't agree with their rendition of the story," Waters informed his boss.

The chief, his attention still on the photos, continued. "He probably didn't fall. Definitely looks like he was pushed, or maybe was hit in the head with the table."

"We believe that's the case, sir," McBayne confirmed.

"Your buddy back home did this?"

"Yes. New gaming software, great for simulations."

The chief pulled out the next sheet of paper from the portfolio Waters provided. He unfolded it and laid it out on his desk, covering most of it. It was a printout of the suspect blocks and relationship diagrams that Waters showed his partner a few days earlier. It was complete with pictures, data sections, and the solid and dashed lines depicting the relationship of the suspects to the victim.

The Chief reviewed the document, then looked up at Waters. "You think these other three couples are involved somehow? And the data supports it?"

"We think they were all at the Spiers' house that night," McBayne added.

"Could just be a coincidence. People can be in the same area at the same time."

"It could, but they all live fairly far apart, so not likely. And the occurrences are very consistent," Detective Waters said.

He took another sheet of paper from Waters' stack and quickly reviewed each transaction, line by line.

Waters leaned over the desk and pointed to parts of the paper. "These transactions place them together almost every Friday for the last several weeks, with a few exceptions. And then there's a void of transactions between seven and around ten."

McBayne continued. "Whatever they were doing appeared to end around ten. Then there're several bar and restaurant charges at that time at local establishments around the Spiers' neighborhood."

"What's this?" The chief pointed to a section of transactions on the bottom of the last page.

"It's a separate trust under Spiers' name, created a few weeks ago. Five deposits of exactly fifty thousand dollars made on the same day, within hours of each other. I could only confirm deposits by three of the five couples. Two I couldn't track the source, presumably Browning and Williams."

"They all deposited 50K to a separate account?" the chief asked.

Waters nodded. "Then there's a withdrawal from the same account of fifty thousand early last week."

"We think that's the return of the Thomas's money," Detective McBayne said.

"Interesting. Now money's involved." The chief rubbed his chin in thought. "Of course, it could be a group investment, some kind of ante or buy in."

"I'm not sure where that money ended up. There's been no deposit in any of the Thomas's bank accounts yet," Waters informed him.

"Where did you get this banking data?" the Chief asked.

"You really want to know?"

He paused for a second. "No, I guess not."

"Well, I do," Detective McBayne said.

Waters looked at her and shook his head.

"Why?"

"Plausible deniability," the chief answered.

"What does that mean?"

"It means we don't go to jail if we get busted. Only he does." The chief motioned toward Waters.

"We should be fine until the bureaucrats are forced to close some privacy loopholes," Waters said.

The chief looked up at the detectives, down at the documents, then back to the detectives. "Well, okay then."

The detectives looked at the him, expecting more.

"Okay what, sir?" McBayne asked.

"Let's get them. Let's find out what really happened to Frank Thomas. I think you're right, something's going on here." The chief's attitude immediately changed. "You know none of this will be admissible, right? You need to get a confession or have a rock solid eyewitness to force a plea bargain. If this goes to court, we lose. You thought O.J. had good lawyers; wait until you see who these people bring in."

The chief paused. "McBayne." He looked her in the eye and spoke in a serious tone. "These aren't street thugs. You can't bully them with your badge and harsh language. They'll laugh in your face and have you sued for harassment."

"Got it, sir."

"You need to outsmart them, think before you say or do anything. If they even have an inkling they're under investigation, they'll lawyer up and you'll never get a thing out of them. I assume you're going to start interviewing all the couples?"

Waters nodded.

"Interview them separately. Chance meetings work best. Don't make appointments and give them time to communicate and figure out what's going on. Do the women first. They're easier to break." He looked at McBayne. "No offense, detective."

"None taken."

"Let's get a tail on Spiers right away. He's the main suspect, right?"

The detectives nodded confirmation.

"All right, let's get to work." They got up to leave the office. "Detectives?"

They stopped and turned around.

"Good job."

CHAPTER 23

Detective McBayne took in every detail inside the house as Mrs. Thomas led them through the living room to the kitchen. There were no family pictures on the wall, no sign of children or much of anything personal. Like her husband's accident, something just didn't seem right.

"How are you doing, Mrs. Thomas?" McBayne asked her, still looking around.

She shrugged.

"I know, it's hard."

The detectives took seats at the large counter in the Thomas's kitchen.

"We just have some follow-up questions about Frank's accident. This shouldn't take long," Waters informed her.

The Thomas home was impressive. The kitchen looked like they could film a cooking show in it. A granite counter top wrapped around a large, six burner gas stove and a copper exhaust fan cover was mounted above it. Expensive pans hung from the ceiling and looked like they had never been used.

Detective McBayne took out her notebook. Waters pulled his phone from his shirt pocket, she could tell he was getting into photographer mode. She put her hand over his phone and gave him a disapproving look and subtle shake of her head—he placed it back in his pocket.

"So, you and Frank arrived at the Spiers' house around seven?" McBayne asked.

"Yes, around then I think."

She was still somber, likely still in shock about the death of her husband.

"And it was just you and the Spiers, no other guest stopped by?"

Jayne paused, looked away from the detective and answered. "No, it was just Frank and me."

"You were downstairs when the accident happened?" Waters asked.

"Yes, in the kitchen with Emma."

"Was Frank acting strangely, anything going on with him out of the ordinary?" McBayne said.

"No, same old Frank. We had a couple drinks, but that never affected him."

"This is a tough question, but we have to ask. Were you and Frank having any issues, personal or in your marriage?" McBayne asked the new widow.

She gave the detectives a curious look. "Why would you want to know that?"

"It's just standard questions," Waters chimed in. McBayne's comforting tone seemed to have rubbed off on her partner.

"What's going on? Is this an open case? Do you not think Frank fell?"

"No, not at all. Why, Mrs. Thomas? Do you think something else might have happened?" Detective McBayne asked her.

Jayne hesitated, her eyes darted from side to side, then she responded. "Have you talked to Ron Spiers about this? He was the only one there when Frank fell."

"Ron was on his way up the stairs when it happened, right? He wasn't on the balcony?" Waters asked.

"If that's what he said, that must be where he was."

"How long did you know the Spiers, Mrs. Thomas?" McBayne asked, changing the subject.

"We met Emma at a charity event. She was trying to help a friend get a children's book published. Frank was helping her with that. They worked together on and off for a few weeks."

"Oh, how nice. Did the book ever get published?" McBayne asked.

"I don't know. I doubt it or they would have mentioned it."

McBayne wrote in her notebook, then looked up at Mrs. Thomas. "Is there anyone we can talk to about that?"

"Frank's partners I guess."

"How often did you socialize with the Spiers?" McBayne continued the questions.

Jayne thought before replying. "Every few weeks since we met them."

"Always on Friday night and at the Spiers house?"

"Um, mostly I guess, yes."

"Did you meet any of the Spiers other friends?" Waters asked.

Mrs. Thomas looked at him. "That's an odd question, Detective. Why do you want to know that?"

Waters looked uncomfortable. "Well, we—"

McBayne cut him off. "I think that's all for now. Thank you for your time, Mrs. Thomas."

They got up to leave. Mrs. Thomas walked them to the door, still looking at them suspiciously.

McBayne turned to her. "Again, I'm sorry for your loss. By the way, my parents did the Alaska cruise, it's beautiful. I know it might be difficult, but you should do it, maybe just to get away."

"What are you talking about?" Jayne asked her.

"I thought you and Frank were planning a cruise?"

"No, Frank hated cruises." Mrs. Thomas looked confused.

"Oh, well. I must have heard that wrong. Okay, we'll be in touch if we need anything else."

They said goodbye and the detectives got into their car. Waters backed out of the driveway and turned to his partner. "What was that about the cruise?"

"Spiers said that's one of the things he and Frank were talking about the night of the accident…looks like someone is lying."

CHAPTER 24

Howard Andrews stood outside of a yuppie bar in the suburbs North of Dallas. He finished his cigarette, dropped the butt on the ground, and crushed it with his shoe. He hit the top speed dial button on his phone that said 'Carrie'. A few rings later someone answered.

"Hey, how are you?... I'm good. Almost settled in...My furniture finally showed up... Never using that company again." He paused and listened for a while, nodding and making facial expressions as if the person on the other end could see him.

"Job's going okay, but it's a weird place... Yeah, I can't get any information from anyone." Another delay while he listened. "They have some odd accounting practices I'm looking into, something doesn't seem right. I might have to report them to the Feds if I don't get answers soon, gotta cover my own ass."

Another pause. "Yes, I've been thinking about it too.... Just not ready to move back in yet.... I think we need a couple months apart, see how things shake out." He listened some more, then the conversation came to an end. "Okay, talk to you soon. Love you." He hung up and entered the bar.

"What'll you have?" the woman bartender asked.

"Yuengling and a shot of whiskey."

"Jack Daniels okay?"

"Sure."

The bartender quickly returned with the drinks like the seasoned pro she obviously was. Howard slid her a credit card. She picked it up and looked at it. "Thank you, Mr. Andrews." She turned and put his card in the cash drawer with the others.

"Do you have Wi-Fi?"

"Yes. It's Clancy's. Password is bigtippers. All lower case."

Howard smiled at the not so subliminal message as he selected the

Wi-Fi entry on his phone and typed in the password. He went to his email program, then checked his text messages, nothing. He looked at the stock market alerts for the day that people in his profession are supposed to monitor, again nothing interesting.

He looked around the bar. It was the typical Wednesday evening crowd; mostly young professionals, not yet married or with children, probably on their way home from downtown Dallas or Ft. Worth after work.

Howard was new in town, looking for a new start. He and Carrie got married a year ago, they definitely pulled the trigger too early, should have lived together for a while. It didn't go well, they got along better on the phone than in person.

He signaled to the bartender for another round. He stared blankly at the TV's ahead of him and periodically took a drink of his beer. Several minutes passed and a woman sat on the stool next to him.

"Is this seat open?"

He nodded.

She was a brunette, probably in her mid-thirties, had a cleaned up, biker chick look. She was wearing dark tinted glasses, kind of peculiar for inside, at night. He looked over at her, why not.

"Hi, Howard Andrews."

"Nice to meet you, I'm Shelly."

"Hi, Shelly. Are you from Dallas?"

"No, just here on business," the woman answered.

That's odd, she didn't look like a business woman. "Can I buy you a drink?"

"Sure."

"What'll it be?"

"Whatever you're having."

"Shot and a beer?" Andrews asked her.

She gave him the why not shrug.

The bartender brought the drinks over as the conversation continued. They got through the opening pleasantries and were in the career discovery phase.

"I'm an accountant." He paused. "Oops, should I have made up a more exciting profession."

"No," she said and laughed. "You're doing fine. Honesty is always the best approach."

"It's been a while since I've done this."

"Done what?" she asked.

"Talked to a woman in a bar."

"Really? Are you trying to pick me up, Howard?"

"That depends, is it working?"

"We'll see," Shelly said. She downed her shot and ordered another for both of them.

Howard was starting to get quite buzzed from the alcohol and lack of food. The conversation started heading down the flirty path. They moved closer together the more personal it got, the side of their legs touching.

They were becoming more and more comfortable together, laughing after every sentence whether it was funny or not and everything started to have a sexual innuendo. He finally leaned over and kissed her. She pressed her body against his, her hand placed strategically on his thigh.

"Do you want to get out of here?" she whispered.

Howard smiled, then signaled for the check. They left the bar and headed out to the parking lot.

"I'm out back," she said and made a motion behind the bar.

He followed her to the overflow parking area behind the bar. The front lot wasn't full, and hers was the only car in the back. She lead him to a white compact in the back corner of the vacant lot. It was dark, there were no working street lights, and the lot was lined with tall trees.

She stopped at the driver's side door and turned around. Howard walked up beside her and pressed his body against her. They started kissing. She let the back of her hand rub against his groin area. He pressed against her harder.

"Well, I didn't expect the evening to proceed like this," he said.

She smiled.

They kissed, more passionately now, grinding their bodies against each other. He opened her leather jacket and slid his hand under her blouse. It made its way under her bra. She suddenly stopped kissing him and looked around.

"No one can see us back here," he assured her.

A sobering chill set in as he felt a presence behind him, like they weren't alone. He pulled his head back and looked at her. Her eyes were fixated on something over his left shoulder, she was trying to hide it, but not very well. He slowly turned around. There was a man standing behind him wearing a black ski mask, he had a wooden baseball bat resting on his shoulder.

Before Andrews realized what was going on, or had time to say anything, the man wound up and swung the bat, catching Andrews solidly in the forehead. It made a gruesome thud. He instantly dropped to the ground, blood flowing from a wide indentation above his eyes.

The woman jumped back, then opened her car door, got in, and drove away.

The man with the bat walked over to Andrews and gave him two more violent blows to the head. If there were any signs of life in him, they were gone now. He reached down, grabbed the wallet out of Andrew's back pocket, and disappeared into the darkness between the trees.

CHAPTER 25

Detective McBayne followed the shapely blonde, Charlene Browning, wife of renowned heart surgeon Dr. Charles Browning, as she entered the main entrance to the North Park Center Mall. Detective Waters was a ways back pretending to talk on his cell phone.

McBayne wore a tight skirt, a blouse that showed off her figure, and high heels. She cleaned up well, could definitely work in an office downtown if she wanted, although it would probably bore her to tears.

The detectives had spent the last couple days trailing the women they suspected were at the Spiers house the night Frank Thomas died—looking for any opportunity to run into them and start a conversation. They hadn't been successful, yet.

They casually looked around the corner as Charlene entered the Apple Store and signed in with a nerdy looking Asian girl holding an iPad. Mrs. Browning took a seat in the large, comfortable seating area in front of the store. Detective McBayne whispered into the ear of her partner, giving him the plan. He nodded, he looked impressed.

McBayne approached the Apple store, keeping her eye on Charlene. The store was busy but there were a couple seats unoccupied beside her. McBayne made her way over.

Charlene was dressed to impress, or rather to attract, wearing a short skirt that required constant attention to keep from exposing her panties. McBayne grinned at the men around them trying to get a glimpse under it without their wives or girlfriends catching them.

"Hello, is this seat taken?"

Charlene looked up at the detective, then shook her head. McBayne sat down.

The detective pretended to check her phone, pretended to look at her watch, pretended she was looking for someone. A few minutes passed and a man walked up to her.

"Hi, Honey," Waters said and leaned down and gave her a kiss on the cheek. It startled her, she didn't realize her partner would know how a husband behaves, and definitely didn't think he could pull it off. He sat in the seat beside her.

She interrupted Charlene. "Excuse me, how long have you been waiting?"

"I just got here, but I had an appointment."

"Me too. I wonder if they're on schedule."

"They're usually pretty good. And it's quick once they get you in," Mrs. Browning replied.

"What's wrong with your phone?" McBayne asked.

"I keep getting this warning that pops up. It says I don't have the right cable. There's not even a cable plugged in," Charlene said and held the phone up proving her point.

McBayne looked at Waters. He was staring directly at Charlene Browning's chest. In his defense, she was wearing a top that encouraged that. "Honey," McBayne said, trying to get his attention; nothing. "Honey, up here. Didn't you have that same problem with your phone?"

Waters looked at her, returning from where ever he was. "Oh yes, I believe I did."

"Do you want him to take a look? He's really smart," she said to Mrs. Browning and shot her pretend husband a fake smile.

Charlene looked at them and thought for a second. Apparently they looked like a harmless couple. "Sure, why not?" She handed her phone to Waters.

Now he was staring down at her skirt and those beautiful tanned legs coming out from under it. Charlene didn't even notice his stare. He composed himself and took the phone from her. He pretended to inspect it, front and back, touching all the ports and controls. Next, he opened the cover, hit a few buttons, went to the utilities section and checked the memory.

Waters angled the phone so Mrs. Browning couldn't see what he was doing. He clicked her calendar icon and quickly noted dates highlighted in the past and in the immediate future. He let out a couple "Hmmm's," as if he'd found something interesting. Then, he went back to the utilities screen and held the phone up for her to see.

"Just make sure you have the latest updates installed. I think you do. Otherwise, it looks good. You restarted it, I assume?"

She took the phone back. "Yes, a few times. Well, thanks for taking a look. They should be calling me soon anyway."

"Honey, why don't we go get a pretzel, I think it's going to be a while," McBayne said. She turned back to Charlene. "We'll be back in a bit. Good luck with your phone."

"Thanks, you too."

Waters and McBayne got up to leave. He was still looking back at Mrs. Browning as they turned and headed down the crowded corridor of the mall.

"What was that all about?" McBayne asked when they were out of range. He shrugged and had a confused look on his face. "If we were really married you'd be in a lot of trouble right now."

"For what?"

"Ogling her."

"Oh, that…she's really pretty," he said as if that wasn't blatantly obvious to anyone who saw her.

"Wow, Detective Waters is human; he notices girls."

They made their way past the standard mall stores; the cookie and pretzel vendors, cheap jewelry merchants, and the luxury car display that you could win just by entering your name. They left through the entrance where they came in.

"Well, anything useful?" McBayne asked him eagerly.

"I think so. She had an appointment set for this Friday at seven pm listed under '5-F-5'."

McBayne thought for a second. "5-F-5, what does that mean?"

Waters shrugged. "No idea. Last Friday, nothing. But then the same label and time were entered for several Fridays before it. Whatever they were doing before Thomas died looks like they're continuing."

"5-F-5. We need to find out what that means," McBayne said.

CHAPTER 26

Detective Waters perused the area surrounding the cemetery. He and McBayne watched as they prepared to bury Frank Thomas.

"Find out where Spiers is," he said to his partner.

"Where's Spiers now?" Detective McBayne spoke into her walkie talkie.

A voice from the black device replied. "Just pulled up, getting out of his car now, the black Range Rover. I think that's him. He's wearing a dark blue, pin-striped suit. The wife is in a black dress. Wow, it's very form fitting for a funeral."

She clicked the button to speak. "Okay, thanks, Murph."

The detectives were parked on a side street away from the road where the cars in the funeral procession were lined, a safe distance as not to be seen. Junior Detective Steven Murphy had drawn the duty of tailing Ron Spiers and was giving the detectives frequent updates. They didn't want to be spotted staking out Thomas's funeral and tip off any of the couples.

Unlike the cop shows, trailing a suspect was exceedingly boring and one of the least desired jobs. It cost the department a lot of money, usually overtime pay, and they rarely produced results and never ended in a wild car chase like in the movies.

McBayne took notes while Waters scanned the funeral site with his binoculars. It was high noon on Wednesday, a week and a half after Frank Thomas's accident. According to the Thomas' Facebook page, the funeral was delayed so Frank's family from New England could make travel arrangements and his brother could get back from serving in the military overseas.

Funeral attendees were making their way from the line of cars parked outside the wrought iron fence surrounding the cemetery. The detectives watched as a top of the line Audi pulled up and bypassed the cars along the road. It stopped, the driver got out, and opened the back door.

"That's Jayne Thomas," McBayne said. "That must be her mother beside her. And the guy in uniform is probably Frank's brother."

"Nice car. I bet Shaun Williams lent it to them for the funeral. Dealerships do that," Waters commented, looking through his binoculars.

Shaun and Sky Williams were behind Jayne in another Audi. They got out and followed Jayne's group to the gravesite. The detectives continued to watch.

"Here comes Jacob and Victoria Daniels," Waters said.

"There's your girlfriend," McBayne said. Waters looked confused.

"Oh, right." He spied Dr. Browning and his wife Charlene walking from the opposite end of the street.

The voice on the other end of the walkie talkie broke in. "Holy shit, you see that? That's how you dress for a funeral."

"Careful, Murph, Detective Waters has dibs on her if anything happens to her husband."

"Okay, that's all of them," Waters said, changing the subject. "Let's see how they interact."

They continued their surveillance as the four couples and the recent widow took seats around the burial site. None of them were sitting together. The front row of guests were seated on white wooden chairs. There were a couple more rows of people surrounding them.

"Good turnout. He must have been popular," Waters commented.

"Look at Emma Spiers," McBayne said.

"What about her?"

"I think she's more upset than Jayne Thomas."

Waters focused his binoculars on Emma. He noticed the man sitting beside her. It was presumably her husband in the dark pinstripe suit, as Murphy informed them. "Look at Ron Spiers," he told his partner.

She focused her binoculars on Ron, zooming in as far as they would go.

"That's not him," McBayne said.

Just then there was a loud wrap on the passenger side window where McBayne was sitting. Startled, they both turned. It was Ron Spiers peering into their car. Waters hit the button to roll down the passenger side window.

"Hello, Detectives," Spiers said, not very cheerfully.

"Mr. Spiers," McBayne greeted him.

"What are you doing here?" he asked.

They hesitated, thinking of a response. Finally, McBayne regained her composure. "Paying our respects."

"With binoculars from a side street?" Spiers replied, not missing a beat.

"Uh, yeah. We didn't want to intrude on the services."

Spiers stood and stared at them for a few seconds. The awkwardness didn't seem to bother him, it did the detectives. He finally walked around the car and headed to the funeral service. The detectives watched him.

"Holy shit," McBayne said as Waters rolled her window back up. She hit a button on her walkie talkie. "Murph, what the hell? That's not Spiers by Emma."

"Yes it is," he answered.

"Look closely."

The walkie talkie was silent for a few moments then Murph spoke, "Holy crap, it's not him. Where is he?"

"He's walking back from our car now."

"Really....that's not good."

"No, it's not," McBayne confirmed. "Well, we're made," she said to her partner.

"What do we do now?" Waters asked.

They both thought for a moment.

"Might as well talk to Emma Spiers," McBayne said.

CHAPTER 27

Detective McBayne was working out on a leg extension machine at the high-end women's gym and spa where Emma Spiers belonged. She was dressed in gym shorts and a tank top with a sports bra underneath. She had a bandana wrapped around her head and was well aware of how much less her outfit costs than every other woman there, including the workers.

She subtly kept an eye on Mrs. Spiers as she progressed through her workout, trying to keep the weight from smashing down from her lack of attention. It was more difficult than she expected.

Emma Spiers was looking good, decked out in tight black workout pants that ended just past the knee. She had a loose t-shirt with a bra barely able to hold her ample bosom in place. A young male health club worker held the punching bag as she went through a combination of punches and kicks, utilizing perfect form. She was breathing hard and sweating but had a look on her face like she was nowhere near quitting.

Finally, Emma took a break from the punching bag and went to a cabinet to grab a towel. When she stopped at the water cooler, McBayne happened to be getting a drink as well.

"Mrs. Spiers," she said, feigning surprise while taking a drink from a paper cup.

Emma didn't seem to recognize her.

"Detective McBayne. We met under the unfortunate circumstances at your house a couple weeks ago."

"Oh, right. Hi. What are you doing here, Detective?"

"Thinking of joining. Time to get back in shape."

Emma gave her a puzzled look. "You're joining this gym?"

"Thinking about it."

"I don't mean to be rude, but you're joining this place on a detective's salary?"

"Well, I might push the free visits until they catch on," she said and smiled.

"Got it," Emma said. "I won't blow your cover. You can work out with me if you want."

"You don't mind?"

"Not at all. I was about to finish my kickboxing routine. Would you like to join me?"

"I don't know a lot about it, but sure."

Emma turned to the young attendant who was working with her. "You can go. I have another partner." He looked disappointed.

Mrs. Spiers grabbed a pair of padded gloves from a hook on the wall and tossed them to the detective. "Put these on. I'll show you what to do."

McBayne pulled on the gloves and followed her to the middle of a large mat.

"Okay, when I punch put your hands up, palms facing out. Keep your elbows bent a little. When I kick, use your forearm to block it. Here, let's go in slow motion."

Emma did a slow right jab. McBayne put her hand up, palm facing out, and she hit it. Next a left cross and the detective put her other hand up.

"Good," Mrs. Spiers said. "Now, if I kick like this, block it with your forearm. Brace yourself or you might lose your balance." Emma leaned back and raised her right leg, McBayne blocked it with her forearm.

"You got it, Detective. Now a little faster."

Emma went into a series of slow jabs and kicks, McBayne blocked them. It looked like a dance routine. She started to pick up speed. The women worked pretty well together.

Emma stopped and got a serious look on her face. "Detective, I don't think you're being truthful with me."

Oh, crap. "Ummm, what do you mean?"

Emma paused. "I think you've done kickboxing before."

"Oh," McBayne answered, relieved. "I may have done this once or twice. So, does Mr. Spiers work out with you?"

Emma looked at her, then gave her a stronger kick, almost knocking the detective over. "No. He goes to work early and exercises at the company gym."

"How is he handling Frank's death?"

"Like he handles everything, pretty much indifferent."

Two quick jabs followed by a right kick. McBayne blocked them perfectly. "Were they good friends?"

"I guess. I'm not sure Ron has any real friends." She dropped her hands and looked at the detective. "Are you interrogating me?"

"Oh no, just sad what happened. Crazy accident."

"Yes, it was," Emma agreed. She stopped kicking and punching. "Okay, Detective, your turn."

Emma put up her hands. McBayne started punching, imitating what Emma was doing. She went slowly at first, one hand, then the other, then quickly started moving like a pro out of habit. *Cool it, Carlie, you're a beginner, remember.*

"First time, you must be a quick learner," Mrs. Spiers said sarcastically.

"This is almost as fun as punching drug dealers."

Emma laughed. "Now try a kick."

McBayne bent down and sprung up leading with her right foot. Emma blocked it with her left forearm. Next, she tried her other leg.

"So, your dream was to be a detective when you were a little girl growing up?"

"No. I wanted to be a park ranger."

"Really?"

"Yes. I wanted to work at Jellystone Park with Yogi Bear and Boo Boo."

Emma smiled. The detective continued kicking and punching, starting to breath heavier now.

"I was crushed when my dad told me it didn't exist. Instead, I became a cop, then a detective."

"You're young for a detective, aren't you?"

"Kind of. I took the test to see how I'd do and a spot opened up. So, here I am."

"Do you work, Mrs. Spiers?"

"I do a lot with charities. And entertain Ron's business associates."

McBayne was breathing heavy now. "I think I need a break."

"Sure, come on. I'll buy you a power smoothie."

The women removed their gloves, grabbed their towels, and headed to the snack bar.

"Two orange, banana, protein shakes please," Emma said to the young man working the counter.

"Yes, Mrs. Spiers."

"Did you know Frank Thomas very well?" McBayne asked Emma.

She didn't answer right away and a sad look appeared on her face. "He was sweet. He was helping a friend of mine get a book published. I don't think it had a chance, but Frank never said that."

"Did you see them a lot?"

"Every other weekend or so. Sometimes we'd meet downtown at a nice restaurant."

"And Mrs. Thomas; what's she like?"

"She's nice enough, I guess. Like a lot of couples, they met at their first job after college, fell in love, or what they thought was love. She wanted to start having children, but Frank wanted to wait."

"Do you know why?"

"Probably the usual reason."

"What's that?" McBayne asked.

"He didn't want to have children with her."

The handsome young bartender slid two orange drinks with fruit on top in front of the ladies. Emma gave him a sexy look and mouthed 'Thank you'. He blushed.

"Were they having problems?" McBayne continued.

"I don't know, no more than any other couple I imagine." She paused. "You know what, I don't want to talk about them anymore."

They continued their conversation but moved on to more trivial issues. McBayne finished her protein drink as fast as she could without getting a brain freeze. "Well, I have to get back to work," she said.

"Oh, that can wait. We need to stake out the massage room first," Emma said and gave McBayne a wry smile.

The detective looked at her curiously and smiled back. *Does she know about the stakeout? Would Ron have told her?*

"James," Emma said, getting the attention of the snack bar attendant. "Can you make arrangements for massages for myself and Ms. McBayne?"

James sprung to life. "Yes, ma'am." He picked up the phone and went to work.

***

Ten minutes later the women were laying on their stomachs, side by side on massage tables. There were two mimosas in wine glasses on the stand between them and two strapping male masseuses were massaging the knots out of their muscles.

McBayne reached down to make sure the bottom of her towel was covering her private parts. Emma seemed entertained by her discomfort. "Relax, they're professionals. So, is there someone special, detective?"

"No, not for a while now. The last one got kind of messy, so I'm taking a bit of a break from romance." *Easy, Carlie, she's not your best gal-pal.*

"Really? That's kind of drastic. You're not taking a break from everything are you? One night stands?"

"Not really my style. Just some things I want to accomplish before I go down that path again."

"I agree, detective. Don't rush it. I got married way too young."

"How did you and Mr. Spiers meet?"

"I was waitressing at a fancy restaurant in downtown Dallas. Ron was there one night for a business dinner, and that was it."

"Really?"

"Yep, I was just out of college, UT Austin. Trying to pay back student loans and get a real job as an interior decorator. Made more money at that place than I ever could have at an office job."

"He came in and rescued you from all of that?"

McBayne looked down at the massage specialist who was getting a little close for her comfort on the back of her thighs. He got the message, she wasn't like his usual customers.

"Yes, swept me off my feet. Well, the hundred dollar tip didn't hurt either. We were engaged after a month."

McBayne took a sip of her mimosa and set it back down on the table. "I could get used to this."

"Yes, marrying a millionaire does have its perks."

The ladies finished their massages. Emma arranged for mani-pedicures before McBayne could sneak away, and Emma wouldn't take no for an answer. They changed into matching white bathrobes and headed to the mani room. *Hey, it's part of the job right.*

When those were done Carlie thanked Emma and went to the

locker room. She opened her locker door and pulled out a towel. When she closed the door, she felt someone standing uncomfortably close to her. It was Emma.

"Oh," McBayne said, a bit surprised. She looked down. The front of Emma's robe was opened and her quite perfect breasts were protruding out. Her thin stomach and entire front side was exposed. McBayne tried to ignore it, but Emma leaned in against her.

Carlie looked up. Before she realized what was happening Emma's lips were pressed against hers. At first she thought it was just a quick peck to say good bye, but it lasted way too long for that, then her tongue gently entered the detective's mouth. Carlie pulled away.

"Mrs. Spiers, what are you doing?"

"Oh, I'm sorry."

McBayne stammered, then said, "Umm, no, it's just…that's not appropriate."

"Sorry, I must have misread the situation."

"I just…I'm not like that."

Emma smiled at her. "Are you sure?"

Carlie took her towel and went to the showers, which thankfully had separate stalls and a lock. She took a quick shower and dressed without drying her hair. It created wet spots on the shoulders of her blouse as she left the spa. Mrs. Spiers was nowhere to be found.

The detective made her way to the parking lot and got into the oldest car there, except for some of the employees who had to park in the outer rows. She started to drive out of the health club parking lot. As she passed by a new Lexus, she noticed a woman in the driver's seat with her head down on the steering wheel. She drove slowly past to see if she was all right. As she went by, the woman raised her head. It was Emma Spiers and she was crying. Detective McBayne turned so she didn't see her.

CHAPTER 28

"So, you think Spiers is on to us?" the chief asked the detectives sitting in his office.

"Hard to say. He saw us, but he didn't say much," Waters answered.

"How did you lose track of him? He doesn't have a body double does he, like all those dictators do?" The chief shook his head. "That's odd. Murphy's better than that."

"No idea," McBayne said.

Waters looked over at his partner, distracted by her perfectly manicured and brightly painted fingernails. She noticed his stare and hid them between her knees.

"Nothing else helpful at the funeral?"

"Not really," Waters answered. "None of the couples mingled or talked. It was mostly the family consoling Mrs. Thomas."

"Might have gotten more info if we could have gone to the wake, but that probably wouldn't have been a great idea," McBayne said.

"And the Widow? Nothing?"

"The night of the accident Spiers told me he and Thomas were discussing a cruise to Alaska the Thomas' were thinking of taking. I asked Mrs. Thomas about it, she didn't know what I was talking about. I think Spiers made that up."

"Interesting," the chief said.

"But, she doesn't know anything or isn't ready to talk yet."

"You talked to Emma Spiers?" the Chief asked Detective McBayne.

"Yes, at her health club. I just happened to be in the neighborhood," she said, obviously sarcastically.

"And?"

"She seemed tense, almost angry when talking about her husband,

and sad when talking about Frank Thomas."

"Really?"

"I think there's something there, but I didn't want to push it. But you know what they say; you can't hide your lyin' eyes."

"What? Isn't that from a song?"

"Yes, she does that sometimes," Waters said.

"The Eagles, right?" the chief asked

"Yes. Well, Eagles. The band's name is Eagles, not *The* Eagles." She stressed the word 'The'.

The chief gave her a peculiar look.

"They prefer to be called Eagles."

"I don't really care what they want me to call them. Good song in any case."

McBayne changed the subject. "Chief, when I was leaving the club, I saw Mrs. Spiers sitting in her car by herself, crying."

The chief cocked his head, presumably not knowing what she meant.

"Women like that, they don't lose their composure, especially in public. I think something is really bothering her."

"Something more than a man dying on her balcony?"

"Yes. I think there's more to it."

"Okay. Is that it then, from the health club?"

"What do you mean?

"Is that it? Anything else happen?"

McBayne became flustered. "No, that's it. What else would there be?"

"I don't know, that's why I'm asking you."

The detective shook her head. The chief and Waters looked at her curiously.

The chief continued, still giving McBayne an odd look. "So, the big news is we think they're still meeting with their Friday night club." He looked down at his notes. "5F5. What the hell does that mean?"

"We think it means Five for Friday. Five couples meeting on Friday, the fifth day of the week. Or something like that. Not sure what the last five really means," Waters said.

"Just because it's in Mrs. Browning's calendar doesn't mean they're still meeting."

"Right. But we need to find out what they're doing if they are,"

Waters said.

"It seems to be the key to this whole thing," his partner added.

"And what do you propose we do, invite ourselves to the party, stake out the driveway?"

"No, we stake out the empty house across the street," Waters suggested.

The chief looked at him. McBayne sat up in her seat. Waters had their attention.

He continued. "That house is empty, for sale by the bank. I think the top floor bedroom would have a good view down into the Spiers house…with a telescope anyway."

"We would need to get access to it," the chief said. "I don't think we need a warrant as long as the real estate company okay's it."

"Here you go." Waters slid a piece of paper across the chief's desk. "Jurgenson Real Estate; that's the phone number and agent. On the back is the floor plan of the house."

"You're thinking we get surveillance up there Friday night? Eyes and ears on the Spiers house?"

"Yes, including myself and Detective McBayne if she wants to come."

"I do," she said immediately.

"Friday is tough. The surveillance team is usually swamped staking out drug deals."

"I have the equipment. If they can drop us off, I can set it up. Detective McBayne and I can do the stakeout."

"That might work. Okay, I'll make the phone calls. Let's plan on it, unless I let you know otherwise."

The detectives got up to leave.

"Detectives, if nothing comes out of this, we have to pull the plug on this one."

They nodded and left the office.

CHAPTER 29

It was nearly four pm on Friday. A white van with the words "McHenry Electric" written across the sides in large print made its way down the road of the Spiers' residence. Detective McBayne sat in the back seat wearing a blue McHenry Electric shirt and matching hat. Her hair was pulled up to not draw attention to her gender.

In the front passenger seat was her partner Detective Waters wearing the men's version of the same shirt. He could pass as an electrician, although a nerdy one.

Driving the van was fourteen-year surveillance expert Hal Cummings. He looked like the all-American dad, not a man in charge of eavesdropping on some of the worst criminals in Texas. He seemed competent and had a calming effect on her, she wasn't as nervous as she thought she'd be.

"Detective McBayne, have you been on a stakeout yet?" he asked.

"Not yet. We sat in Detective Waters' car and watched a funeral, but that didn't go so well."

"This will be better. You get to sit in a nice house and use the telescope. You bring snacks and bedding?" Cummings directed his question to Detective Waters.

Waters patted the bag between the two seats in confirmation. Although not very good at communication, he was always prepared. Between the two of them, she felt assured they'd have everything they needed.

"What happens if someone calls the number on the side of the van?" she asked.

Waters answered. "They get an old answering machine message that says we're out on a call, please call back later."

"So, about the same customer service as most places these days."

"It's a real...well, a real fake company in case someone looks us up," Cummings added. "Sometimes we get bad reviews on Yelp. Most of them are, 'They never called me back.' Which we don't, so that's accurate."

Nearing the house, Detective Cummings reviewed the procedures one last time. "We'll pull up to the garage, close enough so the van blocks the view from the street. I'll get out and open the door. You guys get the equipment into the garage. I'll do inspections, you two get inside and get setup before they get home. Got it?"

McBayne and Waters nodded.

"I'll help you get settled, then I have to get out of here. We need to make sure I'm there long enough like it was a real service call."

"Murph said Spiers is still at work, so we should be good," McBayne informed her partner.

"Usually you have to watch out for nosy neighbors, but not in this area. The houses are far enough apart and back from the road, so that won't be an issue," Cummings said. "The other dead giveaway is three technicians arrive, only one leaves. So, you two hit the floor if anyone's around."

They approached the two houses. The Spiers on the left, the one with the for sale sign on the right. The occupants of the van scanned the Spiers driveway for cars or some sign of life in the house. There was none. Cummings pulled into the driveway of the abandoned house, which proceeded slightly uphill. It was a few feet above the Spiers home which should help their viewing angle.

McBayne looked at the two houses, they were farther apart than she remembered. "We're going to be able to see into the Spiers house from here?"

Waters nodded. "Sure, with the telescope. As long as the angle's right we can see anything."

The gate was already open, probably left that way by the real estate agent. Cummings made his way up the driveway and stopped beside the garage. It was on the right side of the house, out of view from the Spiers home.

McBayne grabbed her bag and slid open the van door, waiting for the go-ahead to exit. She let her more experienced colleagues take the lead.

Cummings got out, keeping his head down as he crossed in front of the van—presumably, so any spectators couldn't get a look at his face. He stood in front of the access panel beside the garage door and lifted the cover. After typing in some numbers, the garage door opened.

McBayne watched him, witnessing first-hand how a professional surveillance expert takes on the persona of an electrician doing his job. No one would have suspected it was a cop under cover. She was tempted to lift her head and eye the Spiers house, but realized Cummings and Waters were resisting that urge, so she did the same.

Waters got out of the passenger side door and looked up at the front of the house, then over to the Spiers. She could almost hear the calculations going on in his head. The large window of the top floor bedroom looked directly over and slightly down to the balcony in front of the Spiers home.

Detective Waters grabbed two large black bags from the van and placed them in the garage. Cummings went to the main electrical box on the far side of the garage and opened the front panel. He touched a few circuit breakers, obviously pretending he was inspecting them.

He worked on the main circuit box for a while, then went outside and walked around the yard to where the underground power lines met the building and inspected them. He walked the length of the power lines with some kind of a machine—pretending to take readings.

Waters and McBayne entered the kitchen from the garage. The house was stripped of expensive appliances and anything of value that could be sold. That was typical with foreclosures. They walked through the living room. The house was bare, no furniture, just well-worn carpets. They continued to the stairs and followed them to the second floor.

The detectives checked all the rooms. The master bedroom was in a good location to view the Spiers' home as they had thought. The upstairs was void of any furniture as well. They would be spending the night on the floor.

They entered the master bedroom. A large window overlooking the front yard was on the far side of the room. They approached it from opposite sides, being careful not to be seen. The window was tinted, which helped prevent anyone from seeing inside. At night, they just needed to make sure they didn't turn on any lights and they should be fine.

Waters placed his two bags to the left of the window. McBayne put her backpack on the right. The wall between the window and the floor was about three feet high creating a perfect spot to set up the equipment.

She watched her partner closely as he unpacked a short, futuristic looking telescope and a tripod. He connected the two and placed the tripod on the floor below the window with the telescope pointing outward. Next, he took out a laptop, connected the USB cable to the telescope, and turned on his computer. A few seconds passed and the screen lit up. It automatically recognized the telescope and started a program to control it.

The detectives sat on either side of the equipment with their backs against the wall, facing the inside of the room.

"This is a digital telescope," Waters said. "It's about as strong as a high powered pair of binoculars. This program controls it and records everything we see." He moved his mouse over a set of arrows on the screen. "It can move in or out, scan left, right, up and down. The screen in the middle displays what the scope is seeing."

"Cool. Where did you get this?"

"I made this one. Well, assembled the parts anyway, and set up the driver to control it with the software."

He used the mouse to point the telescope at the front of the Spiers' house. The view was wide enough to include the driveway.

"When they're inside we'll zoom in on the front of the house, through the windows. It'll be clearer when it gets dark, and as long as they have a light source on inside."

"This is amazing," McBayne said, taking in all the information. "This is all you need to do surveillance?"

He nodded. "There's been a lot of advancements in this field the last ten years. You don't need all the technicians to be on hand and sit there for hours staring into an eyepiece straining your neck. We won't have sound. That would be better, but it complicates things, and you need a different warrant for that."

"You guys all set?" Detective Cummings said. He was standing in the bedroom doorway.

The detectives looked around the room, taking a quick inventory of everything they had.

"I think we're good," Waters said and looked at McBayne for confirmation.

She nodded.

"Okay, I'll see you at eight-thirty tomorrow morning. Same

procedure, meet in the garage and load up the gear. I'll call you as I arrive and confirm there are no prying eyes from across the street."

Cummings headed back down the hallway and down the stairs. He left through the garage just as discreetly as he had arrived; leaving no hint that he left two people and surveillance equipment behind.

The detectives unpacked their gear, bedding, snacks, drinks, and prepared to witness whatever was going on at the Spiers' house on Friday evenings. McBayne had a small pillow and put it against the wall. She laid a blanket on the floor, positioning herself on her side. It was more comfortable than she thought it would be and gave her a good view of the computer screen.

Waters took out a thin sleeping bag and rolled it out on the floor. He used one of his bags as a pillow and sat with his back to the wall, low enough so his head couldn't be seen from the window.

The tripod was between them with Waters' laptop on the floor across from it. The telescope was positioned to target the front of the house. The picture continued to become clearer as the sun set.

***

It was almost six o'clock. An occasional car made its way down the country road, bringing its wealthy occupant home from a long week of making a lot of money, presumably.

Waters snacked on an espresso flavored Cliff Bar and a bottle of vitamin water. McBayne brought hummus, whole wheat crackers, and vegetables. They glanced down at the computer screen occasionally to make sure they didn't miss anything as they waited for the Spiers to return home.

"I could use some of your famous coffee right now."

Waters reached into his bag and took out a thermos and two plastic coffee cups, the kind used by campers. He filled each with coffee. Next, he opened two disposable cream containers and poured them into his partner's cup. He looked at her. "A little sugar, right?"

She nodded. He poured part of a packet of sugar in, stirred it with a spoon, and handed her the cup.

"I should have known," she said and took a sip. Now this was definitely better than the stakeouts she'd seen on TV. "Waters, what did you mean about the data and plausible deniability when we were talking to the chief? Are you breaking the law?"

He thought for a moment. "Um, right now the legal precedence for a lot of this personal data is up in the air. You can't go anywhere or do anything these days without generating a transaction, an electronic trail, or cookies on a website." He paused and took a drink of his coffee.

"Well, big companies and government create that data and they want to use it. They think it's theirs. But civil rights groups say it belongs to the individual and it's an invasion of privacy to use it. Right now the big business lobbyists run the show. They have the money and they own the politicians. So, they're going to use it.

"So, we have access to most of that data, and we use it when we need to. But if it ever came to a trial or lawsuits, their lawyers would eat us alive. Or at the very least tie it up in court for years. For now, we quietly use the data, but just to generate other clues."

"I don't want you doing anything that can get you in trouble, okay?" she said.

"We should be good. Just have to be careful with this group. They're smart and they have expensive lawyers."

They continued with small talk, eating their snacks, and checking email on their phones. Forty minutes passed, then Emma Spiers Lexus pulled off the road into the driveway. They both sat up. McBayne jotted the time and subject in her notebook.

The garage doors opened and her car disappeared into it. They watched the windows and doors on the front of the house for any movement. It was still too light out to see much of anything inside the house.

Waters dragged the mouse over the zoom button and hit the plus sign. The telescope zeroed in on the balcony and glass doors leading out to it. They could see the balcony and doors clearly and part of the sitting room on the other side of it. He adjusted the focus until it was as clear as he could make it. An image appeared on the balcony.

"Look, that's her, right?" McBayne commented.

He focused the frame on Emma standing on the porch.

"What's she doing?"

"I don't know, just standing there, looking down," Waters answered

"That's the spot where Frank Thomas died, right?"

He nodded.

The second garage door opened distracting them from Emma.

Waters zoomed back out to the wider view. A black Range Rover pulled up the driveway.

"That should be Ron," McBayne said and wrote in her notebook.

The SUV disappeared into the garage and the door closed behind it. Waters panned back out to the shot of the balcony. Emma Spiers was still standing there. A few minutes passed and they saw a man enter the balcony and stand beside her. They were both looking down at the same spot.

"And that's Spiers," Waters said.

The couple appeared to be talking and getting more and more animated.

"Are they arguing?" McBayne asked.

"I think so."

On the computer screen, they watched as Ron Spiers grabbed Emma by the front of her blouse. He pulled her close to him and tried to kiss her. She turned her head. He pushed her back then slapped her across the face.

"Holy shit," McBayne said. "What was that all about?"

Emma left the balcony. Ron remained for a few seconds, then exited through one of the glass doors as well.

The two detectives were speechless. They looked at each other with helpless expressions.

"Christ, what do we do now?" McBayne said.

"Nothing we can do, unless she's in grave danger… and I don't think she is."

McBayne scribbled down some notes. Waters zoomed the telescope back out so they could see the driveway. They waited for the other guests to arrive.

CHAPTER 30

Almost an hour had passed when an Audi pulled into the driveway and parked at the very end where it started to wrap back around. Waters moved the telescope over to the car. Two people got out, an older man and a beautiful blonde.

"Try to contain yourself," McBayne said to Waters.

He was confused.

"Charlene Browning."

"Oh."

Charlene and the doctor walked to the front steps. Dr. Browning carried a small bag over his shoulder. They opened the door and entered, not waiting to be let in.

There was no activity on the balcony or sitting room behind it. Waters zoomed in on the front door of the house. "Look down the hallway into the living room," he told McBayne. "I think I see movement down there."

"Hard to tell, but I think you're right. If they stay in that room we're not going to see much."

Another car pulled into the driveway, a silver Chrysler 300. It stopped behind the Browning's car and a young couple got out.

"That has to be the Daniels," Waters said.

Victoria Daniels had an overnight bag along with her purse. They walked up the stairs. Just like the Brownings, they opened the door and entered.

"And our final couple is coming now," McBayne said as another Audi with dealer plates pulled into the driveway and parked behind the Chrysler. Two people exited.

"Shaun and Sky Williams," McBayne said and wrote the information down on her notebook.

Shaun had a backpack hanging over one shoulder.

"I wonder what's in those bags," Waters said.

"Not sure. You wouldn't bring wine or food in those, I wouldn't think. Maybe they're staying overnight."

Waters checked his watch, it was seven forty-three and starting to get dark. The telescope view inside the house was becoming much clearer.

"All right, all four couples have arrived. Let's see what they're up to," McBayne said, keeping her eyes on the monitor.

A few minutes passed. Waters panned over and zoomed the telescope into the balcony as far is it would go without the picture becoming blurry. They could see fairly well into the sitting room, but not much beyond that. Below, through the glass of the front door, they could see into the living room, but the images weren't clear.

The view into the sitting room was broken into segments from the four glass doors of the balcony, making visibility more difficult.

"We have activity," McBayne said.

Two women wearing white bath robes came upstairs and entered the room. They had a stack of white sheets and towels. They put them on a side table, took out one of the sheets, and unfolded it.

"What are they doing?" Waters asked.

"Looks like they're covering that ottoman with a sheet. I think that's Emma Spiers and Victoria Daniels."

More people entered the room.

"They're all wearing white bath robes," McBayne said.

Everyone was now in the room and could be seen fairly clearly through the balcony doors. McBayne tried to take notes and not miss any of the action on the screen.

"Can you make out who's sitting where?" she asked her partner.

Waters squinted to focus on the screen. "The chair on the left is Ron Spiers. Couch has Emma, then Victoria and Jacob Daniels. On the loveseat is the Williams. Charles Browning is on the big chair to the right, Charlene is sitting on the arm."

McBayne wrote down the info.

The couples sat and talked for a while. Finally, a man stood, went to the middle of the room, and sat on the ottoman. He faced the front doors of the balcony. His body was partially blocked where the two middle doors met.

"That's Shaun Williams," McBayne said.

Charlene Browning walked from her chair and stood in front of

Williams. Her back was to the balcony doors. She made a motion to Emma Spiers, who then appeared to hit a button on her phone.

Charlene dropped her robe to the ground, exposing her perfect boat model body. She was wearing a light blue bra and panties. Williams took off his robe and placed it to the side. His muscular body was completely nude seated on the ottoman. He leaned back and braced himself on his arms.

Charlene spread her legs a little and her right arm dropped down to her midsection. She moved her body slowly, seductively.

"What the," Waters said, stopping himself before he swore.

McBayne looked at him. "This should be interesting."

"What's she doing?" he asked.

"I don't know, dancing for him? Can't tell with her back to us. He seems to like it."

A few seconds passed. "I think she's rubbing her tits and her other hand is in her panties," McBayne said and took a quick glance at her partner. He looked puzzled. "Touching herself."

Waters wouldn't look at her.

Charlene reached behind her back and unsnapped her bra letting it fall to the floor. She moved forward, closer to Williams. It looked like she was lifting her tits with her hands and pushing them together.

Several seconds passed and she moved closer and leaned down in front of Williams. Her arm started moving up and down. Her body blocked the detectives' view.

"I think she's jerking him off," McBayne said.

Another minute or so passed and she stopped. She leaned in closer to him and lowered her tits over Williams lap. She started moving her chest up and down.

"Titty fucking," McBayne informed her partner before he could ask.

"Really?"

"I don't know what else it could be."

The couple continued that for a minute, then Charlene slid her head down to his waist and it began to bob up and down. She turned her body and they could see his penis in her mouth.

"And that would be a blow job," McBayne said and wrote some notes on her pad.

They did that for just under a minute. Shaun Williams' head rolled back and his body become more animated. Charlene stopped, stood up, took off her panties, and straddled Williams. The detectives could see her ass perfectly through the glass windows, bouncing up and down on top of Williams. She rode him a few times, then stopped. Neither of them moved for a few more seconds.

Emma Spiers got off the couch and handed Charlene a towel. She climbed off Williams, stood, and placed the towel between her legs. She put her bra and panties back on, then her robe, and walked back to her place on the chair beside her husband. Charles appeared to give her an approving nod.

"Okay, that was interesting," Detective McBayne said and took some more notes.

Williams was lying back on the ottoman, not moving. Eventually, he got up, put on his robe, and returned to his place on the love seat beside his wife.

Detective McBayne glanced at Waters. He had a look of complete bewilderment and still wouldn't make eye contact with her. The show on the computer screen continued. Emma Spiers and Victoria Daniels took the sheet off the ottoman, tossed it to the side, and replaced it with a new one.

Finally, Waters spoke. "I don't know if we should be watching this."

"Too late now," McBayne said, still writing. "You okay?" She looked at him and smiled. He blushed and didn't respond. "You've never seen a live sex show?"

"No," he said definitively.

Jacob Daniels left the couch, dropped his robe, and sat on the ottoman. Emma Spiers walked to the spot in front of him. She sat on the floor, untied her robe, and opened it, but didn't remove it completely. The rest of the people sitting around the room looked more interested now.

Emma started moving her legs and hips slowly while sitting in front of him, giving him brief glimpses of what was under her robe. About a minute passed and she stood and let her robe drop behind her. She had a shapely body, good muscle tone, and her athletic shoulders made a nice V shape down to her hips.

Next, she laid on the ottoman beside Daniels. Whatever she did on the floor had him fully erect. She took his penis in her right hand and started moving her hand up and down. The detectives could see what she was doing clearly. She was off to the side so her back wasn't blocking their view.

"Well, that's pretty obvious," McBayne said.

After about a minute Emma stopped, leaned over him with her chest suspended over his waist, and let her tits hang down. She rubbed them against his stiff penis, alternating between lightly touching him with her nipples, teasing, then pressing her chest firmly against his penis.

Another minute passed and she dropped her face over his lap and took his penis into her mouth. Her hand cupped the base of his cock, massaging it. Daniels' eyes closed and he bit his lower lip.

Several seconds passed and she stopped. Daniels stood and Emma took his place on the ottoman. She sat down and spread her legs. He stood between them and leaned into her, grabbed behind her knees, and wrapped her legs around his waist. The detectives could only see his naked backside moving up and down, obviously fucking her.

He did that enthusiastically for close to a minute, then he stopped, his body collapsing on top of her. Victoria Daniels stood, grabbed a towel, and walked over to them. She handed the towel to Emma while her husband climbed off her.

Jacob stood and put his robe on. Victoria reached up, put her arms around his neck, and pulled his head down. She gave him a long, passionate kiss. Daniels returned to his spot on the couch. As he sat down, Shaun Williams reached over and gave him a high five.

McBayne laughed, "I wonder what that's all about."

"Maybe they're teammates," Waters said.

She looked at him, stunned. "Was that a joke?"

He shrugged, apparently it was.

Sky Williams, easy to spot because of her strawberry blonde hair, and Charlene Browning changed the sheet on the ottoman this time.

"At least they're practicing good hygiene," McBayne said.

Charles Browning got up, disrobed, and took his turn in the middle. The detectives could clearly see the smile on his face.

Victoria Daniels moved to the spot in front of him. She took off her robe, exposing her thin, sleek body. She laid beside him, without touching him. With her right hand, she cupped her breast and brought it to her mouth. She began licking her nipple while staring seductively at the doctor.

He watched her and became immediately erect. She slid her other hand over her perfectly trimmed bush and continued until her fingers were between her legs. Her face was near the doctor's face, licking her lips.

Next, she licked her hand and started stroking his penis, his grin got even bigger. After a minute passed she slid under him, helping him maneuver on top of her. She pulled his waist up to her chest and put his penis between her tits. She pushed them together while he moved his hips up and down. They did that for another minute.

"I'm starting to sense a pattern," Detective McBayne said and continued taking notes.

Victoria slid down on the ottoman, pushed him up, and took his penis into her mouth.

Waters and McBayne could only see his backside with her hands grasping his ass, pulling him toward her. This didn't take long. The doctor's body trembled, and he fell onto the ottoman. Victoria moved out of the way so he didn't land on her.

Emma Spiers stood and handed Victoria a towel. She put it to her mouth, spit into it and wiped her chin. She put her robe back on and took her place on the couch beside her husband Jacob.

Emma and Charlene changed the sheet this time.

"They're very efficient," Waters said.

McBayne smiled. "Yes, that's one of my takeaways from this as well."

The last couple approached the center of the room. Ron Spiers had been sitting in his chair expressionless. He slowly walked to the ottoman, looked around at the other people, and dropped his robe to the ground. He was in great shape for a man approaching fifty and walked as if he knew it. He sat toward the front of the seat like he was waiting to be entertained.

Detective McBayne, trying to take notes and watch the action, took another look at her partner. He was still watching but didn't look quite so bewildered now, in fact, he looked bored.

On the screen, they saw Sky Williams leave her husband on the love seat and move into position in front of Ron. She dropped her robe to the ground. She was wearing black underwear; bra, panties, and nylons held up by garter straps connected to her panties. The other men in the seats smiled as she exposed her undergarments.

She started moving her hips slowly and sexy. She took off her bra, staring at Spiers the entire time. She bent over, unsnapped her garter, and gave him a good view of her tits as she rolled down her stockings. Ron appeared more amused than aroused.

She finished undressing, then turned around and bent over, looking out the balcony windows directly into the telescope. Her ass was inches away from Ron's face. He nodded and smiled.

Several seconds passed and she turned back around and knelt in front of him. He leaned back. Sky started rubbing his penis. She did that for about a minute, alternating between fast and slow. It didn't seem to have much effect on him.

She leaned over him, her ass positioned perfectly in the telescope frame and let him fuck her tits like the couples before them.

Another minute passed, she stopped and put her face over his groin, resting her arms on his thighs while her head moved up and down over his lap. She moved fast then slow, sometimes just the tip of her tongue touching him, then taking him in as far as he could go.

They stopped and switched places. She bent over the ottoman, sticking her ass out and looking over her shoulder at him. Ron moved forward and entered her from behind. She shook her ass as they moved together in rhythm, her arms braced against the ottoman, Ron pulling her hips toward him aggressively. This continued for a minute, then they stopped. Sky turned her head and looked back at him. He smiled and nodded, looking more evil than passionate.

He reached out and Emma squeezed something from a tube into his hand. He moved in closer to Sky and reached between her legs. He grabbed his penis and maneuvered it into her, then gave her a violent thrust, slamming her down into the leather ottoman. She held onto the piece of furniture as he moved faster and faster, pounding her against it with each thrust.

Ron seemed to be looking at the love seat at Sky's husband, Shaun Williams. Shaun turned his head and didn't watch. About a minute and a half passed and Ron's body shook, then stopped moving. He pulled out. Everyone in the seats surrounding the ottoman looked disappointed. He grabbed his robe and put it back on.

Sky rolled over on the ottoman. Emma Spiers came over with a towel and sat beside her. Victoria Daniels handed her robe as Sky cleaned herself up.

Everyone in the room stood and looked to be talking amongst themselves. The women grabbed the towels and used sheets. They all headed downstairs.

"I think that's it," McBayne said.

The detectives continued to watch. They saw some movement through the front door down the hallway and into the living room. Waters adjusted the telescope for a better view. He moved it down and over, in and out, but it was no use, they must have gone into the interior rooms of the house.

***

Twenty or thirty minutes passed when four people left the house from the front door. It was Charlene and Charles Browning and Shaun and Sky Williams. They waved goodbye to each other, got into their cars, and drove away.

A few more minutes went by and Jacob and Victoria Daniels left the house and got into their car. They made their way down the long, circular driveway and onto the old country road. When they were out of the frame, Waters focused back onto the house.

He scanned the downstairs, moving the telescope side to side, checking all the windows; nothing. He guided it up to the top floor. Lights were on in the back side of the house, probably the bedroom. He moved the telescope to the balcony, zoomed in as far as it would go, and scanned from left to right. At the far end of the balcony, something came into focus. He and McBayne realized what it was, Ron Spiers. He was standing on the porch smoking a cigar, looking right at them, his head filling up most of the monitor.

"Shit," McBayne said and slid down to the floor as if he could see into the room.

Waters thought for a minute. "He can't see us. We're too far away."

"Then what's he looking at?"

"I don't know. There's no light or anything on the telescope by design."

"That man is creepy. Let's take the scope down."

"No, that he might see."

They continued to watch Spiers on the balcony in the computer screen. He finished his cigar, seemed to be smiling into the camera, then turned and walked away.

McBayne and Waters watched the screen for several minutes. There was no more activity. They were both exhausted, physically and now mentally from five hours of stakeout work. She grabbed a plastic water bottle from her bag and took a sip, then looked over at Waters. He was still staring at the computer screen.

"Was that an orgy?" he asked her without looking up.

"I don't know. I thought everyone had sex at the same time in an orgy. That looked too scripted like they were on a schedule."

"What was the last thing Spiers was doing with Sky Williams?"

"I think it was anal sex," she said with a tone like she was breaking bad news to someone.

"Sex in the rear end?"

She nodded.

Waters thought for a minute. "Is that normal?"

"For some people, yes. But it's considered pretty kinky."

He hesitated, then asked, "Have you done that?"

McBayne was uncharacteristically embarrassed, but nothing Waters said would surprise her at this point. She thought for a second. "A guy tried that with me once. And I'll tell you what, he couldn't bend his wrist for a month."

"He put his whole hand in there?"

"No, what's the matter with you! I bent his hand back when he tried it."

"Oh."

"You better get explicit approval before trying that."

They both smiled and let out a stress relieving laugh. Waters shook his coffee thermos. It was empty. He grabbed his vitamin water bottle and took a drink.

"Would you like some carrots and hummus?" she asked him.

"Sure. I could use a shower too."

McBayne laughed. "Yes, that was dirty."

She slid the Tupperware container over to him. He helped himself. They continued to sit with their backs against the wall thinking about what they just saw. McBayne broke the silence. "Well, that was interesting, but not sure it helps our case much."

"No, we still need to find out what happened to Thomas."

All the lights were off at the Spiers house now. The detectives were lying flat on their backs with their heads on their pillows. They continued talking, occasionally checking the telescope monitor.

"It might be time to get more aggressive," McBayne said.

"What do you mean?"

"Start interviewing all the participants. Put pressure on them to talk. See what we can drum up."

He gave her the 'why not' shrug.

McBayne took out her earbuds, plugged them into her phone, and turned on her music. Waters could hear it, an Eagles song of course. He laid his head down, closed his eyes, and drifted off to sleep with Don Henley's unmistakable voice singing 'Best of My Love.'

The next day they woke up as the sun rose. They did another scan of the house with the telescope, there was nothing going on. They packed their gear and moved their bags down into the garage and waited for their ride. At eight twenty-five they got a call from Cummings saying all clear. A few seconds later the garage door opened.

They quickly loaded the van and headed down the driveway. Stakeout over.

CHAPTER 31

Sky Williams answered the door. "Hello, you must be the detectives."

"Yes, I'm Detective McBayne. This is my partner, Detective Waters."

She shook their hands and invited them into the house. "Nice to meet you. You had a question about Frank Thomas?"

"Yes, we're working the case," McBayne answered.

"Working his case? He had an accident, didn't he? Why would anyone be working his case?"

"Yes, he did, Mrs. Williams. But there's been some new…findings. Some of the evidence we gathered doesn't make sense. We did more digging and it's revealed some issues."

"Issues?"

"We don't think Frank fell; we think something else happened to him."

"Really? Like what?" Sky led them into the living room, they took seats on a small couch. Sky sat in a chair beside them.

"We're trying to find that out," McBayne said. "Mrs. Williams, we know you and Shaun were at the Spiers' house that night. And we know the Brownings and Daniels were there, too."

The detectives were silent, trying to gauge her reaction. Sky looked at them for a moment, then picked up her phone from the coffee table in front of her. She hit one of the speed dial buttons, waited a few seconds, then started talking. "Hi, Candice. I need to talk to Shaun right away." She waited another few seconds, glancing up at the detectives. "Okay then, tell him to call me as soon as he's free. It's important." She put the phone down and looked at the detectives.

Detective Waters spoke. "Mrs. Williams, if you've done anything illegal, you shouldn't be talking to us and you should get a lawyer immediately."

Sky looked stunned. "What does that mean? I haven't done anything."

"Okay good," he continued. "Now, if that's true, you should answer all the questions we're about to ask you as honestly as you can. You'll be on record as cooperating—meaning you don't have anything to hide. Do you understand?"

She nodded.

"Let's go then," McBayne said and took out her notebook. "So, you acknowledge you were at the Spiers house the night Frank Thomas died?"

She nodded.

"Where were you when you heard him fall?"

"I was in the kitchen."

"And where was your husband?"

"Shaun? He was with me. Well, he was coming in from the living room right after we heard the crash."

"Are you sure?" Detective McBayne asked.

"Yes, of course."

"But, he wasn't with you when you heard the fall?"

Mrs. Williams thought for a second. "Just after it."

McBayne looked at Waters. They had anguished expressions. "Should we tell her?" she asked him.

Waters thought for second. "It's up to you."

"Tell me what?"

"Listen, Mrs. Williams, I shouldn't be telling you this, but they're thinking about issuing an arrest warrant for your husband," McBayne said.

"For Shaun? Why? He didn't do anything."

"I know but, well, I'm sure you can guess why."

"Because he's black?" she said more as confirmation than a question.

McBayne paused. "I can't confirm that. But, he can't conclusively account for where he was at the time of the accident and everyone else can."

"I just told you he was in the kitchen with me. And what do you mean everyone else can?"

"Well, you said he wasn't in there yet, right? Also, he's big and strong enough to kill someone. And he does have a previous record."

Waters gave his partner a surprised look, then quickly tried to hide it.

"Previous record, that juvie thing? He spray painted his name on a bridge when he was thirteen. Are you kidding me?"

"Well, it's in his record, you know?"

"Those sons of bitches. Racists, that's what they are."

McBayne shrugged in subtle agreement. Waters was silent, watching his partner work. She was becoming a pretty good detective... or a pretty good liar.

Sky continued. "I know how this works; pin it on the black man. And once they get him in the system he doesn't come out, right? Case closed."

"We can't comment on that, Ma'am," Waters said, joining the charade.

"Did the others put it on Shaun? Is that what this is about? Are they trying to save their own asses?"

"I can't discuss what other witnesses have said." Detective McBayne said. "If you can just explain a few things to us, I think we can stop the warrant."

"Explain what?"

"Well, first of all, we know about the five for Friday meetings."

"Five for Friday? You mean five for five?"

"Oh right, five for five," McBayne said and wrote in her notebook.

"What do you know about it?" Sky asked.

"We know everything. That the five couples have been meeting at the Spiers house the last few Friday evenings for....well, you know."

Waters watched her reaction. She didn't seem embarrassed or concerned.

"So, you already know all about it then. What do you want from me?"

"Well, we need you and Shaun's version of it to compare with the other couples. What it is, how it's done? There are some things we're not clear on."

"But Shaun's not here."

"That's okay, you can speak for him."

Sky paused, looked at her phone, then at the detectives. "Well, it's a sex game. Five sex positions in five minutes. Whoever lasts the longest without ejaculating wins."

"Five sex positions?" Waters asked.

"Yes. Hand, tits, mouth, pussy, ass."

"So, just to clarify, hand is?" McBayne asked her.

"A hand job."

"And tits are?"

"Titty fucking. Girl have you had sex before?"

"Yes, ma'am, I have."

"How about him?" Sky motioned toward Waters. "Does he need me to draw a picture?"

"He might," Detective McBayne said as both women looked at Detective Waters. "I'm just kidding, no pictures. Continue please."

"Mouth is a blowjob, pussy is in the vagina, and ass is anal sex."

"And how long have you been playing this game?"

Sky thought for a second. "Well, it started out just having sex with your spouse in front of everyone and comparing times. Then we started swapping couples. Then Ron suggested we have a real contest, rotate partners, and play for money. So, I guess we're in week four. Oh, we skipped the week after Frank died."

"And how many weeks does it go for?"

"Five. You fuck everyone once, then end with your spouse."

"And what happens with the Thomas' since Frank died?" Detective Waters asked.

"Oh, we just skip their turn. And their points from before don't count."

"Points?" McBayne said.

"I thought you knew all this." Sky looked at them suspiciously. "The men get a point for every second they last and don't come. If they make it the whole five minutes they get a bonus minute. It's the women's job to get them off as quickly as they can, and hopefully before they get in your ass."

"That's right," McBayne said, nodding knowingly and writing down more notes.

"Just five minutes?" Waters said.

"Hey, it's not easy. Five minutes in five different holes. With your friend's hot wife and her husband watching. You ever try it?"

Waters shook his head.

"Oh, and they get a minute warm-up, too."

"Minute warm up?" McBayne said.

"The women get a minute to warm up their partner for the night.

You know, do sexy stuff to get them hot. You can't touch them, though. You play with yourself, strip, take off your underwear real sexy; that's what I like to do."

"What are the white robes for?" McBayne asked.

"Oh, that's just how we start out. So everyone looks the same, and it's faster to get to the sex that way. You don't have to undress."

"And whoever has the most points at the end wins?" McBayne asked.

"Yes, total points, plus bonuses, after five weeks."

"And what do they win?" Waters asked.

"Two hundred and fifty thousand dollars. Every couple put in fifty thousand to play."

"How do you know when times up?" Waters asked.

"Someone has a phone with a timer. They just say *time* after a minute. It's usually Emma unless it's her turn."

Sky's phone rang. She looked at the number, then answered it.

"Shaun, two detectives are here, they're asking about Frank's death. They don't think it was an accident. And they know about five for five." She paused and listened for a while. "I don't know. Okay, I'll tell them."

She hung up and looked at the detectives. "You have to leave now."

***

The Detectives were in Waters' car driving out of the Williams' neighborhood. They nodded to the well-dressed gatehouse attendant as they left the gated community.

"Well, that clears up a lot of the mystery," McBayne said.

Waters nodded.

"We need to get the rest of them into the station house ASAP before they organize and lawyer up."

Waters looked over at his partner. "How did you know Shaun Williams had a juvie record? I can't even get that data."

McBayne smiled. "I didn't."

CHAPTER 32

Over the course of the next two days, McBayne and Waters brought in all the participants for questioning, except the Spiers and Jayne Thomas. They refused. The couples wanted to be questioned together, but the detectives insisted that that wasn't going to happen.

The interrogation room at the precinct was more comfortable than one would expect. It was designed to be pleasant and encourage people to cooperate, not intimidate them. Detective McBayne opened the questioning to each participant with the following statement.

"We know about the game, we know about the money, we know you were there the night of the accident. We don't care about any of that. All we're trying to find out is what happened to Frank Thomas.

"You are not a suspect. If you answer all our questions truthfully, keep the lawyers out of it, we can keep this story from leaking to the press. If we catch you lying or you refuse to answer, we can't promise that. Do you understand?"

***

"First question, how did you meet the Spiers?"

Charles Browning
"My wife, Charlene, and Emma Spiers worked some charity together. They got friendly and Emma invited us over for drinks one night. Then it became a regular thing."

Jacob Daniels
"Ron's my boss. The boss asks you to come over for drinks, you come over for drinks."

Shaun Williams

"Through Charles Browning. He buys all his cars from my dealership. His wife and Emma Spiers were friends."

***

"Why did you play the game?"

Charles Browning

"It's what people like us do."

Charlene Browning

"Charlie wanted to play. Look at me; he's obviously going through a midlife crisis. Plus he wanted to hang out with the cool kids. He wasn't very good, never even lasted long enough to get to the fucking. He knew he wasn't going to win.

"For me, having sex with four hot rich guys and my husband doesn't care, why not? I think Charlie got off watching me, too. Sometimes I'd stare at him while I was getting fucked or giving a blow job. It's pretty hot. You should try it sometime."

Jacob Daniels

"I'm not sure. Ron and Emma just slowly acclimated us to the idea. Every weekend they'd take it a little further. First just drinks, then hot tubbing. You get drunk and play spin the bottle, then truth or dare. Next thing you're making out with your boss's wife. Then you're screwing."

Victoria Daniels

"If you want to have a house like the Spiers someday, you play the game, right?"

Shaun Williams

"I don't know. Sky wanted to do it. I didn't care. She's enough excitement for me. But once you start playing it was fun. And, of course, you want to try to win."

Sky Williams

"Shaun knows I love him, and only him. Anything with anyone else is just physical. Why not? Why not do what you want, what feels good, because of some bullshit morality forced upon us by a bunch of religious hypocrites?"

***

"Who was winning?"

Charles Browning
"Not me."

Charlene Browning
"Frank. He was a machine."

Jacob Daniels
"Frank. Ron was a close second. I was third, but I'm not going to beat Ron. That wouldn't be a good career move."

Victoria Daniels
"I'm not sure, probably Frank. Jacob was right up there."

Shaun Williams
"Frank, then Ron. Those boys have some stamina."

Sky Williams
"Frank. He was unbelievable. He could make pornos if he wanted."

***

"What was the interaction like between Frank and Ron?"

Charles Browning
"Same as anytime two alpha males meet. Only one's going to survive."

Charlene Browning
"They were competing. One of them was going to win. Everyone

else was playing for third place."

Jacob Daniels

"Ron's the big dog. I'm sure he thought he could win easily. But Frank was giving him a good run. Ron isn't used to coming in second. I'm sure he didn't like that."

Victoria Daniels

"I could sense a lot of tension between them. Frank was beating him at his own game."

Shaun Williams

"It was a great showdown. Like two great boxers going at it."

Sky Williams

"I think they hated each other. But they never let it show. They were too composed for that."

***

"On the night Frank died, did anything unusual happen?"

Charles Browning

"Not really. I had my best night. Took Victoria Daniels to three twenty-eight."

Charlene Browning

"I had Ron that night and got him off. I'm sure he didn't like that. Of course, he was already in my ass at the time. Frank gave Emma an orgasm. That was the big news. That was pretty amazing, and Frank gets a bonus minute for it. That was a good show. Emma usually makes all the guys come pretty quickly. She's sexy, I might have a go at her sometime."

Jacob Daniels

"Frank had sex with Emma that night. But Ron's not the jealous type, so I don't think that mattered. It was a pretty good show. Those two went at it."

Victoria Daniels

"Yes, lots of tension that night. Frank got Emma off. It was actually kind of beautiful. I thought they were going to kiss, but that's definitely not allowed."

Shaun Williams

"It was my turn with Jayne Thomas. Longest I lasted. But nothing else that I can think of."

Sky Williams

"Hell, yeah. Frank and Emma put on a show. They came at the same time. Unbelievable, especially with all those people watching. I'm not shy, but I don't think I could have an orgasm in front of them."

***

"Where were you when the accident occurred?"

Charles Browning

"Let's see. I got dressed downstairs, then went into the living room. I was over by the corner, on my phone, had to check in on a patient. You can check my phone records if you want to verify it."

Charlene Browning

"In the bathroom off the kitchen cleaning myself up."

Jacob Daniels

"Living room, checking email and voicemail on my phone."

Victoria Daniels

"Downstairs in the kitchen with Jayne and the Williamses, I think."

Shaun Williams

"I was walking into the kitchen. I had just changed clothes in one of the back bedrooms."

Sky Williams

"I was in the kitchen."

***

"What did you do when you heard the crash?"

Charles Browning

"Finished my phone call. Then Ron started calling for me to come upstairs to the balcony. I did, checked on Frank. He was already gone. Must have died immediately. There was nothing I could do."

Charlene Browning

"I didn't really hear it. I came out of the bathroom and everyone was upstairs. So I went up, too. That's when I saw Frank. So sad. He was a nice guy."

Jacob Daniels

"I heard it, hung up my phone, and ran right upstairs."

Victoria Daniels

"We all went upstairs. Sky and Shaun, me and Jayne."

Shaun Williams

"Headed upstairs with the rest of them."

Sky Williams

"Victoria, Shaun, and I went upstairs. And Jayne, too."

***

"Why didn't you stay for the police and EMT's to arrive?"

Charles Browning

"I wanted to, but Ron convinced us it wasn't necessary. And, of course, it would come out about the game. I'm a nationally recognized heart surgeon. I don't need that kind of publicity."

Charlene Browning

"Ron said to leave. There was nothing we could do."

Jacob Daniels

"Ron told us to go."

Victoria Daniels

"Ron said leave."

Shaun Williams

"Ron said he, Emma, and Jayne would handle it. There was nothing we could do. No sense in dragging us all into it and have to explain what we were doing there."

Sky Williams

"Ron said he would handle it."

***

"Where was Emma Spiers when the accident happened?"

Charles Browning

"I have no idea. She was already upstairs when I got up there."

Charlene Browning

"I'm not sure. I assume she was in the kitchen with the rest of them. Or maybe the living room."

Jacob Daniels

"Emma? Bathroom, I think."

Victoria Daniels

"I think she was in her room changing."

Shaun Williams

"Not the living room. Or the kitchen. I'm not sure."

Sky Williams

"I don't know. She wasn't in the kitchen with us."

***

"Why did you keep playing after someone died?"

Charles Browning
"Most of us wanted to stop, but Ron said we would lose our money."

Charlene Browning
"I left it up to Charlie. We were enjoying it. I didn't want it to end. And what could we do to help Frank. He was gone."

Jacob Daniels
"Stop? Why? We gave Jayne her money back."

Victoria Daniels
"There was only one week left, so no sense in stopping now."

Shaun Williams
"I wanted to stop. I told Ron that, but he threatened to leak the game to the press if I quit. I couldn't afford that. I'd lose my job."

Sky Williams
"Shaun wanted to continue. That surprised me. I thought he would end it immediately."

CHAPTER 33

The chief stared at the two detectives sitting in his office. Putting them together was one of the strangest decisions he'd made as the head cop—mostly because he had no idea how it would work out. He knew there were very few people who could work with Detective Waters, and McBayne was a completely untested resource with a reputation for being too aggressive and not following procedure.

So far it was working out. Waters was getting cases closed and McBayne hadn't gotten herself in trouble...yet. Best of all, he knew he didn't have to worry about them becoming romantically involved, which was the downfall to a lot of mixed gender detective partnerships.

He sat stunned as they detailed their latest findings in the Thomas case and couldn't hold it in any longer. "The men get a point for every second they don't what?"

McBayne nodded. "Yes sir, you heard right."

"And the winner gets the two hundred and fifty thousand dollars?"

"Well, two hundred thousand now that the Thomas' are out," Waters corrected him.

"Holy shit. Now I can retire, I've definitely heard it all."

Wonder how long I would last with the old lady. He thought for a moment, putting himself into the game. Back to the case. "So, you got the Williams woman to cave pretty easily, then the rest followed?"

"Yes, sir," McBayne said. "I don't think the others know anything about what happened on the balcony. They all volunteered to be interviewed without their lawyers and answered all the questions."

"You agree?" he asked Detective Waters.

"Yes. They'd have lawyered up if they were guilty of anything."

"Right, probably trying everything they can to keep it out of the press. And everyone confirmed where each other was when the accident happened?"

The detectives nodded. "The only question is where Emma Spiers was when Thomas died. No one seemed to have an exact location," Waters said.

"And the Spiers won't talk?"

"No," McBayne said. "Why would they? They have nothing to gain by talking. They're the only ones who could get in trouble for lying to the police."

The chief nodded in agreement.

"I think there was something going on between Emma and Frank. All the witnesses, well, mostly the women, said the sex between them the night Frank died was unbelievable. Lots of passion. They wanted to kiss. They even had an orgasm at the same time."

"Impressive," the chief said and thought for second. "Could be...money and passion—the two biggest reasons people kill each other." He pondered whether to muddy the water even further. He had to tell the detectives. "Okay, here's something to confuse the situation further."

He slid a picture across his desk to the detectives. They leaned forward. It was a photo of a dead man lying in a parking lot with his head caved in. The detectives looked up at him. "That's Howard Andrews. Head of accounting at Taylor Financial. Well, the former head of accounting."

"Ron Spiers company?" Detective Waters asked.

"Yes. They found him a few nights ago outside of Clancy's Bar in West Dallas.

"Any suspects?" McBayne asked.

"A woman came in and had a couple drinks with him. They left together. A dishwasher found him later that night in the parking lot out back."

"And they can't find the woman now?' Waters asked.

The chief shook his head.

Both detectives were lost in thought, presumably trying to figure out how Spiers accountant might be connected to the case.

"Can I get the file on this?" Waters asked.

"Sure, Detective Jones is in charge of that investigation, ask him for a copy...and work together on it, " the chief said and gave Waters a long stare. "Together," he repeated.

Waters nodded.

"Okay, detectives, this is all interesting stuff, but we're no closer to finding the truth now than we were two weeks ago, right?"

"Correct," McBayne said, "unless we know what happened on that balcony, we're kind of stuck. One of the witnesses is dead and Ron Spiers isn't going to say anything. Unless someone else saw something or knows something, we're at a dead end."

"Jayne Thomas was definitely in the kitchen when it happened?" the chief asked.

They nodded.

"I would question her again, especially now that we know about the game. Push her a little about her husband and Mrs. Spiers."

The two detectives stood and started to leave the chief's office. The chief looked at McBayne. "Maybe you could run into Emma Spiers again."

McBayne nodded and they left the office.

CHAPTER 34

"Mrs. Thomas, we know about the game," Detective McBayne informed her in a calm, comforting voice.

They were back in the Thomas' kitchen where they interviewed her two weeks ago. She looked at them without expression. "Yeah, and?"

"We know three other couples were there the night of Frank's accident," Waters added, "Charlene and Charles Browning, Shaun and Sky Williams, and Jacob and Victoria Daniels."

Detective McBayne watched her reaction closely—still a blank stare.

"It just brings up more questions when people aren't honest with us, we need to keep looking until we have the truth. Especially when someone dies."

Waters continued. "We don't think Frank fell. We think something else happened on that balcony."

"Like what?"

"We're not sure. We're trying to find that out," Detective McBayne said. "Listen, we don't want to tarnish Frank's memory or embarrass anyone, but we need to know what happened. We owe Frank that much, don't you think?"

Mrs. Thomas nodded and took a deep breath. "I don't know what happened on the balcony. When I got up there he was already dead."

"We know. Is there anything else you can tell us? What was the relationship like between Frank and Ron?"

She hesitated for several seconds, then spoke. "Frank just wanted to beat Ron. That was all. Those guys are.... were, competitive." She looked embarrassed and turned away, appeared to work up some courage, then continued. "In bed...Frank could last as long as he wanted. He had complete control. Ron wasn't going to beat him."

"The other couples, Mrs. Thomas, they said the game got pretty passionate when Frank and Emma were together." She watched Jayne closely, again, no reaction. "They said it was like they were making love, that it meant more to them."

Jayne shrugged, looked down, her eyes began to water. "Frank's family... they were just regular working class people. Everything he had, he earned himself. He went to Harvard to learn how those people act as much as to get a degree. But he was never one of them. He wasn't happy when he became a huge success and had everything.

"He loved running a successful company, liked living in a big house and driving a nice car. But more than anything, he loved his friends, his family, his employees. And they loved him. I don't think being rich and successful was what he expected. You have to be competitive to be that successful, and he was. Something about Ron pushed him over the edge."

She wiped away a tear. Detective McBayne reached out and put her hand on her shoulder. Jayne looked at her.

"I think it was Emma. He wanted to beat Ron for her. I think they were having an affair...I never caught them, never saw an email or text to confirm it, and he never admitted anything. It's just a feeling." She took a tissue from a box on the counter and dried her eyes.

"They started working on that book together, meeting and talking about it. They told me what they were doing, didn't hide it. Well, Frank doesn't do that with clients. That's not his job. Hell, they don't even publish children's books."

"Why did you and Frank play the game, Mrs. Thomas?" Detective Waters asked.

McBayne looked at him, it didn't sound like a Chance Waters question or tone.

"They seduced us. Emma seduced Frank, Ron seduced me. Ron can be convincing and charming when he wants something. I imagine he always gets what he wants. We started coming over for drinks after we met. Then they slowly worked on us, getting more flirtatious, more explicit, talking about how fun it would be to swap couples. You only live once, why not do the things that feel good, that line. But we never gave in, that is until Frank agreed to play."

"Why did you agree to it?" McBayne asked.

"To save my marriage," she said, her voice cracking as if the act of speaking the words was painful. "I wasn't doing it for Frank anymore; in bed, intellectually, in conversation. If having sex with a bunch of different women could get him off, I was willing to allow that. And maybe watching me with other men might spark something in him. I'd even take jealousy."

McBayne gave her a sympathetic smile.

"The second week of the game I was matched with Ron. He took me all five minutes—pretty easily. I don't think I came close to getting him off. And he stared at Frank the whole time he was screwing me. And Frank stared right back at him.

"I felt like I let Frank down, but I don't even know if he cared. He never said anything. That's when I knew it wasn't just Ron versus Frank."

A tear rolled down her face. She grabbed another tissue from the box on the counter. "Then that last night, when Frank was with Emma. They made love. They weren't just screwing and playing beat the clock like the rest of us. It wasn't a game to them, the way they touched, the way they looked at one another. It was as if no one else was in the room.

"Our sex life was good, but never like that, not even in the beginning. Everyone could feel the passion between them. No one could get to Emma, none of those guys. She got them all off, and pretty quickly. But Frank gave her an orgasm, and he had one too. He had won, right there. Ron couldn't match that."

Her voice faded, she could barely speak. "And I knew I had lost Frank forever. I lost him twice that night in one hour."

She regained her composure and looked up at the detectives. "I have no idea if Ron had something to do with Frank's death. I just knew my marriage was over."

The detectives finished their questions, more details about where and when. They didn't gather much more information from her. They did confirm that Ron gave Jayne back her fifty thousand dollars. Finally, they conveyed their condolences again and made their way out of the house.

CHAPTER 35

Detective Waters pulled into the reserved parking spot in front of his apartment. His partner's Mustang drove past him and found an open spot on the road. It was dark. The sun had set about an hour before and the street lights were on.

The two had planned on working late—update some data, review accident scene photos, see if there were any clues they were missing that could break open the case. Although there had been some interesting developments, they were still no closer to finding out what happened to Frank Thomas. Waters was also working on the Howard Andrews case. There had to be a connection to Ron Spiers, detectives don't believe in coincidences.

Waters waited for his partner on the sidewalk. He watched as she approached. "Did you eat dinner?"

"No, I had a late lunch, why?"

"I thought maybe we could order out. A lot of people get Chinese food I believe."

She let out half a laugh. "Yes, I believe a lot of people do that."

"There's a place down the street."

"Is it any good?"

He shrugged.

"Let me guess, you've never been there?"

"Well, I picked up a menu, just in case."

They entered the building. Something was different. Waters realized the light in the entry way was out again. It would likely be another month before it got replaced unless he did it himself, which he's done in the past. The maintenance team only did repairs every six weeks and it drove him crazy.

He led the way up the staircase. Just before they got to the top, a dark figure appeared in front of them. It was a man wearing a gray sweatshirt with the hood up, the shadow hid his face.

The stranger panicked when he saw them and barreled into Detective Waters. He fell back into his partner, knocking her backward. Waters caught himself on the rail with his right hand, but she fell down the stairs, landing on her shoulder then her hip.

The intruder flew downstairs and smashed into the door, pulled it open, and ran away. Waters rushed to the bottom of the stairs to check on his partner. She was conscious, but in a lot of pain, holding her shoulder.

"Are you okay?"

"Yes, I think so. Follow him." She made a motion toward the door.

Waters left her and quickly went outside. He looked to the left, then to the right and saw the man running down the sidewalk. He felt his anger swell as he chased him down the street and thinking of his partner laying at the bottom of the stairs.

The man turned right at the next block. When Waters got to the corner, he saw a car peeling out and drive away into the darkness.

"Shoot," he said and kicked a garbage can beside the driveway.

Detective McBayne was sitting up against the wall at the bottom of the stairs when he returned. He helped her to her feet. She was holding her back. He tried to help her up the stairs, but she grimaced every time he touched her shoulder.

They got to the apartment door. It was already open, the lock was broken. He reached in and turned on the light, looking around to make sure no one was there. He got Detective McBayne to the couch and helped her sit down. She looked over his shoulder into the dining room where his computers were. She pointed to get his attention.

All of his computers and monitors were smashed. It looked like someone took a bat to them. They looked a little closer, and there was, in fact, an old wooden bat lying on the floor by his desk.

He went down the hallway and looked in his bedroom and the bathroom to make sure everything was all right in those rooms. Waters returned and went into the kitchen and took two frozen vegetable packages out of the freezer, grabbed a couple dish towels from a drawer, and brought them back to his partner.

She leaned forward and lifted the back of her shirt. He could see her stomach and the bottom of her bra. He was embarrassed and tried not to stare. He wrapped the frozen packs in the towels and placed one of them on her lower back where he could see a red mark.

"Right there?"

She nodded.

He did the same with the other pack and lodged it between the couch and her shoulder.

"How's that?"

"Good."

"Okay, just rest like that for a while." He knelt beside her. "Can you lift your arm?"

She tried. "Yes."

"Do you want to go to the hospital?"

She thought for a second. "No, I'll be fine. I don't think anything's broken."

Waters went into the dining room and looked at all the broken computer equipment. Then to the kitchen and looked around. "Good, they didn't smash my coffee maker."

"What about your computers? They destroyed everything and all you're worried about is your coffee maker?"

"Yeah, they don't make this series anymore."

He went over to the closet door just off the living room and opened it so she could see inside. It had floor to ceiling shelves and several computers and monitors stacked on them. "I have extras of all that."

She smiled. "I should have known. But, what about your programs and the data?"

"Oh, that's automatically backed up four times a day in a remote location. I can get all that back. It'll take a few hours, though. Do you want something to drink?"

"Water would be good, thanks."

He went into the kitchen, grabbed a glass, and filled it with ice, then water from his refrigerator. He walked back to the living room and handed it to her.

"Holy shit, this really happens? Your apartment got ransacked? I thought that only happened in the movies."

"Oh yeah, you're not a detective until you've had your place tossed," he said nonchalantly.

"This has happened before?"

"No, I'm kidding. This is the first time. I wondered what that would be like."

"Do you think this is related to the Thomas case?" she asked and took a drink.

"I don't know. I don't think they stole anything. I doubt they hacked into my system. But he didn't look like a teenager just out vandalizing."

"If Spiers is behind this, there's no telling what he's capable of. Is he getting desperate? Are we getting close to discovering something?" Detective McBayne said.

Waters shrugged. He thought about the Andrews murder and now the stranger in his apartment. He looked at Carlie sitting on his couch, injured. For the first time since he met her, she looked vulnerable, almost helpless. He didn't like seeing her like that.

She rested at his apartment for an hour. They tried to figure out who and why someone would break in and destroy his computer equipment. They couldn't come up with a good reason or suspect. No one, except the chief, even knew about the system.

Eventually, Waters drove her home and helped her upstairs into her apartment. He sat outside of her place in his car for most of the night, not sure what he was expecting. When the sun came up, he drove home and started cleaning his apartment.

CHAPTER 36

Detective McBayne fiddled with the coffee mug on the table in front of her. Across from her was Emma Spiers, looking as elegant as ever. She liked Emma, in another time and place, they could have been friends.

Detective Waters sat in his car outside of the coffee shop. She could see him peering through the windows from his car. He was better at stakeouts when he had a telescope. He was also on the lookout for Ron Spiers. His tendency to appear out of nowhere, along with the ransacking of Water's apartment, had the detectives on edge.

"Thank you for meeting me," Detective McBayne said to Emma.

The two women sat at a table in the corner of one of the few coffee shops remaining that weren't a Starbucks or Dunkin Donuts.

"You didn't want to meet at my club?" Emma asked.

"No, they frown on detectives getting free massages and pedicures while on duty."

Emma smiled and took a sip of her chai tea.

"Does Mr. Spiers know you're here?" McBayne asked.

"No, he doesn't. But he'll find out."

McBayne watched the cold expression on her face as she said that nonchalantly. "You're going to tell him?"

"No, but he'll find out. He always does. What do you want to talk about, Detective?"

That was a bit unsettling. "A few things. First of all, we know about the game." She paused. Emma's facial expression didn't change. "I assume you know we've interviewed everyone except you and your husband?"

Emma nodded.

"They were all forthright with information. We just can't seem to place where you were when Frank had his accident."

Emma thought for a second. "I think I was coming out of my room. I had just finished getting dressed. There was a lot of commotion at that point. We all just rushed to get upstairs."

"Was there any animosity between Frank and your husband?"

"I don't think so. They both wanted to win. That's who they are."

"Why did you play, Mrs. Spiers?"

She paused. "It was Ron's idea. If Ron wants something, he's going to get it. I helped get the players and convinced them to play. It's what I do."

"And who was winning?"

She took out her phone, hit a few buttons, and looked at the screen. "Well, let's see, Frank was until he died. And now Ron is."

"What's that?" McBayne asked.

"It's the spreadsheet that I keep score on."

Holy shit. "Oh, um, can I get a copy of that?"

"No, but you may look at it." Emma handed her phone to the detective.

McBayne looked at the screen showing a miniature spreadsheet with all the players on a grid. The men's names were listed across the top. Along the side it said weeks one through five. Each cell under the man's name contained the woman they were with that week and two numbers separated by a colon beside them.

"What are the numbers?"

"That's how long the men lasted. Minutes and seconds. Their total is at the bottom."

The detective was trying to analyze the numbers and memorize the sheet before Emma took the phone back.

"If they went the whole five minutes, they get a bonus minute. That's what the plus one means."

"Frank had two fives. Until he was with you." McBayne said and looked up at Mrs. Spiers. "You finished him off just under four minutes."

Finally a reaction. She nodded.

"You seemed to finish everyone off pretty quickly."

Another shrug. "What can I say? I know how to please a man."

McBayne looked at the bottom of the sheet at the totals. Ron was way ahead with Frank out of the contest. "So, Ron's going to win?"

"Of course he is."

"Mrs. Spiers—"

Emma cut her off. "Call me Emma."

"Emma, can I show you a picture? We have some questions we hope you can answer."

"Sure."

Detective McBayne picked up a folder by her purse and pulled out a full page photo. She placed it on the table in front of Mrs. Spiers. It was a picture of Frank lying on the balcony dead. She watched Emma's reaction.

Emma glanced at it for a second then turned to the detective. "Yes, what's your question?"

"See where the table is?" McBayne said and pointed to it on the photo.

"Yes."

"If Frank accidentally fell back and hit his head, it should be lying somewhere over here." She pointed to a spot about three feet from Frank's head. "Not way back behind him where we found it."

"I wasn't very good at physics, Detective. Why are you asking me this?"

"Just wondering if you might know what we're missing. You were first on the scene after Ron, right?"

She nodded.

"Did anyone move it? Maybe slid it out of the way?"

"I don't know, I didn't. Maybe Ron did."

"But he won't talk to us, will he?"

She smiled and gave her an of-course-not shake of the head.

"What kind of table is that anyway? I don't believe I've seen anything like it."

"We picked it up in Italy on our honeymoon in a town just north of Naples. It's a lovers table, designed to hold two glasses of wine."

"Ironic it ended up killing a man, don't you think?"

"I don't know what you mean."

"It broke up your lovers game."

"I wouldn't call us lovers. And it's not over."

McBayne brought her attention back to the photo. "So, Frank is lying here and this is the injury to his head." She pointed to it. "We think he fell backward and hit his head here. It's just difficult for that table to end up over here. That's what our lab is telling us."

Emma's eyes were fixated on Frank. "I don't know what to tell you, Detective," she said, still locked on Frank's face, her voice sounding different, a little sad.

"You admired him?"

She nodded. "He was a really good guy."

"Emma, I have to ask you something. Were you and Frank having an affair?"

She didn't appear surprised or offended by the question. "No. We were just friends. We were meeting a lot. He was helping get my friend's book published. But, we weren't romantically involved. Well, except for three minutes and fifty-four seconds in week three." She motioned down at the spreadsheet and smiled.

"Emma, can I tell you something? I know what it's like to be in an abusive relationship. There is help. You can get out. If you ever need anything, please call me. Or if you just want to talk. You have my number, right?"

Emma nodded. She took a drink of her tea, then looked at McBayne. "Detective…I married Ron knowing who and what he was. It's kind of hard to blame someone after the fact for being exactly who you knew they were."

"Okay," McBayne said. "Is there anything else you can tell me about the night Frank died?" She looked down at the photo again trying to get Emma to look at it.

She didn't and shook her head no.

"Okay then. Well, I better get going. Are you going to be all right?"

"Yes, I'm always all right."

The detective stood, put her hand on Emma's shoulder, and started to walk toward the door. She moved slowly from where her back was injured the day before.

"Detective?" Emma said.

McBayne stopped and looked at her. "Yes?"

"Never mind."

The detective turned and left the coffee shop.

Already Gone

	R.Spiers	S.Williams	C.Browning	F.Thomas	J.Daniels
Wk 1	Victoria (4:21)	Emma (2:32)	Sky (3:12)	Char (5:00+1)	Jayne (3:55)
Wk 2	Jayne (5:00+1)	Victoria (3:05)	Emma (1:49)	Sky (5:00+1)	Char (3:21)
Wk 3	Char (4:47)	Jayne (3:17)	Victoria (3:28)	Emma (3:54)	Sky (3:47)
Total	15:08	8:54	8:29	15:54	11:03
Off	(Frank Deceased)				
Wk 4	Sky (5:00+1)	Char (3:05)	Victoria (3:17)	Jayne (Swap)	Emma (3:51)
Wk 5	Emma	Sky	Char	Jayne	Victoria
Total	21:08	11:59	11:36	N/A	14:54

CHAPTER 37

"Is this chair new? It's comfortable," Detective McBayne asked her partner.

"Yes, I picked it up at Office Depot on the way home."

"You bought a guest chair?" Of all the weird Chance Waters actions, this was near the top.

"Well, you never know when people are going to stop by."

She looked at him suspiciously. "Right, you never know when people are going to stop by to watch you work on your computer. That must happen a lot." She smiled at him. He ignored her.

"It'll be easier on your back than that thing." He pointed to the wicker kitchen table chair she usually uses.

She stared at him, kind of speechless as she realized why he bought a new chair.

"What?" he said, obviously unsettled by her stare.

"Nothing."

"Okay, plug this into that port." He handed her a cable and pointed to the back of some device to the right of the desk. She did.

His computer system was almost back to where it was before the break in. They were just finishing testing connectivity and some of the components attached to the computers.

He hit a few buttons and the machine lit up. "It works."

"Glad I could help," she said and leaned back in her new chair, making a face as her back muscles reminded her they were still sore.

"You're a good assistant," Waters said.

They continued working, making sure all the programs were installed and started up. Waters clicked on an icon and the program with the relationship diagrams of Frank Thomas, the Spiers, and the other three couples opened.

There was more data now and links attached to their profiles and new categories like "motive" and "cleared." Some of the boxes were filled in, some had question marks. Jayne Thomas was no longer identified as a suspect. Ron Spiers was now in dark blue as the primary suspect. Emma was a lighter shade of blue. The rest had been eliminated as suspects and were labeled as witnesses.

McBayne looked at the display, then reality set in. "All this data, all this work, and we're still no closer to finding out what happened to Frank, are we?"

Waters shook his head. "No. Everyone's a major suspect when you're playing a game for a quarter of a million dollars and the guy who's winning it dies."

"You don't think anyone killed him for the money, do you? Isn't fifty thousand dollars to these people like a hundred dollars to us?"

"Maybe. But they still aren't used to losing and obviously don't like it. All right, computers are back up and running. That's good enough for tonight. It's getting late. Do you want some coffee? I have decaf, too."

She thought for a moment. "No, something stronger."

"Stronger, like Espresso? I don't have a machine."

"Not like that stronger. Do you have a beer?"

He shook his head. That's what she thought, but it was worth a try.

"What kind of a bachelor doesn't have a beer? How about Vodka?"

"I only have one bottle of alcohol. You're not on painkillers are you?"

"No, I don't take pills. My mom was addicted to over the counter drugs, so I avoid those. What kind of liquor do you have?"

"I'm not sure, I think it's Tequila. Want me to get it?"

She nodded eagerly. This should be interesting.

Waters crossed the room to one of the kitchen cabinets and opened it. He reached to the back, pulled out a bottle, and brought it over to his partner. "Whoever had this apartment before me left it here. I don't know if it's any good."

"That's Mezcal!"

"Yeah, tequila. Right?"

"Mezcal isn't tequila. Well, technically it is, but it's different.

Tequila is made with Blue Agave. Mezcal is made with Espadin. And they're brewed in different parts of Mexico."

"How do you know that?"

"Holy crap, I know something that Chance Waters doesn't? I told you, I was a bartender for two years. Listen, when I do a job I give it my all."

He nodded. "That you do."

"I don't think it's any good. And there's a dead worm in the bottom, too."

"That's not just any worm. That's *gusano rojo*, red worm. They use those for a reason."

"They put a worm in there on purpose?"

"Yes. And if you make it to the bottom of the bottle and eat the worm, it makes you hallucinate, see things. Some say it puts lead in your pipe."

Waters looked confused.

"Starch in your shorts." He was still lost. "For Christ sake, it gives you a raging hard on."

"Oh," he said and blushed.

"You really are adorable in all your sexual innocence...Let's have a drink."

"No thanks, you go ahead."

She opened the bottle, smelled it, it seemed okay so she took a swig. She immediately made a painful face and coughed a little. It's been a while since her hard drinking days.

"How is it?"

"Great," she said in a rough voice.

"I can tell."

"Detective Waters, is that sarcasm?" She held the bottle out to him. "Now you try it."

"That's okay."

"Come on, what are you, a pussy?" *Oh crap, did I just call Chance Waters a pussy?*

"Really? Peer pressure, that's how you plan on getting me to try it?"

"Well then, what will work?"

He thought for a second. "Try this; 'Detective Waters, would you join me in a drink of an alcoholic beverage'?"

"Okay, Detective Waters, would you join me in a drink of an

alcoholic beverage?"

He hesitated. "Call me Chance."

This was weird, he was being unusually playful. "Okay, *Chance*, would you like to join me in a drink of an alcoholic beverage?"

"Sure." He took the bottle from her, sniffed it like she did, put it to his lips, then took a swig. He made no face at all. "Not bad," he said and put the bottle back on the desk.

She looked at him in disbelief. "You didn't drink any."

"Yes, I did."

"No one drinks Mezcal without making a face. Do it again."

"Okay." He picked up the bottle.

She took it from him before he could raise it to his mouth. She needed proof. He could be a tricky bastard when he wanted to. "No, wait." She opened his desk drawer, grabbed a felt tip pen, and marked the level on the bottle. "Now try," she said and handed it back to him.

He raised it to his mouth and took a couple gulps, again making no face, and placed the bottle back on the desk. She leaned down to eye level where she made the mark. The liquid was about an inch below the black line. "Holy shit, Waters, that's like three shots!"

He shrugged. Obviously, he had no reference if that was a lot.

"Seriously, are you a closet alcoholic?"

"No, I've had two beers my whole life, never tequila. I mean, Mezcal." He placed his hand on his cheek. "My face feels funny. Is that normal?"

"Yes, good, it's working. Let me know when you're buzzed, I want to ask you something."

"Ask me what?"

She grabbed his shoulders and turned him so he was looking straight at her. She paused, was this a good idea?

"Are you ready?"

"I guess."

"Okay." She took a deep breath. This could likely end their relationship, whatever that was. Finally, she just blurted it out. "Chance Waters, are you a virgin?"

He immediately blushed. "Come on."

She watched him closely, he took it better than expected. She pushed a little more. "Just tell me."

He shook his head and looked away.

"You are, aren't you? Are you? Come on, tell me." She knew she sounded like a teenage girl, but it could be blamed on the alcohol.

He looked her in the eyes and asked, "Why do you care?"

"I just want to know. Has any woman, or man, that's fine too, gotten to the brilliant Chance Waters?" *Jesus, Carlie, 'or man' come on. This conversation's over.*

He looked at her curiously. "You think I'm brilliant?"

"Yes… Now virgin, yes or no? Yes or no? *Yessss or nooo?*"

Waters thought for a second. "What about you?"

"Me?" she said surprised.

"Yes, are you a virgin?"

She laughed. "No… See how easy that was?"

She took another drink and handed him the bottle. He did the same.

"Yeah, I didn't think you were."

"Hey, I should be insulted by that. Not really. Hell, I'm twenty-seven years old. It would be weird if I wasn't." She looked at him, realizing he likely could be a virgin. "I didn't mean that. It's fine if you're still a virgin at twenty-seven or even thirty-three is fine. You're saving yourself for marriage. That's cool." *Great save, Carlie!*

"How old were you?" Waters asked her.

"When it happened?" She took another drink of the Mezcal. "I was nineteen."

"Nineteen! I was expecting you to be much younger."

"What's that supposed to mean? Now I am insulted."

He ignored her fake outrage. "With who?"

"My first college professor."

He started laughing. He was definitely buzzed. She smiled as he laughed uncontrollably. Chance Waters was always in control.

"Okay, now that makes sense."

"And now you're laughing at me, Waters. You must be drunk. Another shot of Mezcal for that."

She took a drink from the bottle, made another painful grimace, and handed it to him. He took a big gulp, again no reaction.

"How the hell do you do that?"

He gave her the "I-don't-know" shrug.

"Alright, now your turn," she said.

"My turn for what?"

"Are you a virgin?" she asked. *Was he purposely trying to aggravate her?*

"I don't want to play this."

"No, you have to. Come on, I told you."

"Stop."

She reached out and started tickling his sides. "Are you ticklish? Tell me or I won't stop."

He grabbed her hands. "Dammit, I said stop it."

She realized from his grip and tone he was serious. His jaw was clenched. She hadn't seen this side of Waters before.

"I think you should leave now," he said and released her hands.

They were both silent. She wasn't sure what to do. "Okay," she said and got up to leave. "I'm sorry. I didn't realize it was such a big deal." She gathered her things, looked at him, then turned to leave. She moved slowly, her injured back and shoulder had stiffened up from sitting that long. The alcohol didn't seem to be helping her balance either.

She reached to open the door.

"I'm not a virgin," he said.

She turned to look at him.

"I've had sex, with a woman. One time in high school. And it was horrible and I've never talked about it."

He had an odd look on his face. She wasn't sure if it was just from the alcohol. She returned to the dining room, set her things on the desk, and sat down. "I'm sorry. You don't have to talk about it. I shouldn't have pushed it."

He took another swig from the Mezcal bottle and looked her in the eye. "It was my junior year. I didn't have a lot of friends, as I'm sure you've figured out. I had a crush on this girl, her name was Heidi. She was cute, not cheerleader cute, regular girl cute, like you." He made a motion toward her.

She smiled, that was easily the best compliment he'd ever paid her.

"She was older and beautiful. I couldn't take my eyes off her. Someone had a party and invited the whole class, so I got to go to that one. I knew she would be there or I probably wouldn't have gone. Well, they had alcohol there and everyone was drinking, so I had a beer. And it gave me some courage.

"After a while, she came up to me and started talking. All her friends were giggling. I'm sure it was weird, I had never talked to a girl at school before, I knew they used to make fun of me. Then she asked if I wanted to go to one of the bedrooms and make out. I said yes. Never would have done it without the beer. So, we sat on the bed. It was dark, she started kissing me—I kissed her back. I was self-conscious and nervous, but I liked it."

He took another drink from the Mezcal bottle and continued. "She took my hand and put it under her shirt. It felt nice. I'd never touched a girl there before." He made a motion toward her chest. "Then she unzipped my pants and she laid back on the bed. Her skirt came up and I could see her underwear, the sexy kind. She looked really pretty in the light from the window.

"I couldn't believe I was there with her. She pulled me down on top of her, kissed me even harder. Then she put her hands in my underwear and took out my..." He paused. "Well, you know. She started rubbing me between her legs, then she slid over her underwear, and that was it. It was in.

"It felt... really good. I was overwhelmed and it didn't take long. Then, the door flew open, the lights came on, and all her friends were standing outside laughing and cheering. I was mortified, humiliated. She sat up and said, 'Thanks, Chance, I needed that one'."

"Oh my God, what did you do?"

"I got up and ran home." He paused and took another sip of Mezcal. "They were playing some game to see who could have sex with the most virgins."

Carlie could barely speak. "Shit, shit. I'm sorry. That's the saddest thing I've ever heard."

"Whatever. That was a long time ago, I'm over it now."

She leaned in and put her arms around him, pulling his head against her chest, her chin resting on his head. "No, you're not. No one would be. But that's okay."

He pulled back and looked at her, her eyes started to tear up. "Why are you crying? It happened to me, not you."

"Chance?" she said in a soft, sweet voice.

"Yeah?"

"I'm going to drive to Shreveport, find that Heidi bitch, and kick her right in the twat."

He laughed. "You can't do that."

"Oh, yes I can."

"No, you can't. She lives in Memphis."

They both started laughing, then stopped. They looked at each other, neither one seemed sure what to do next. They were still sober enough to realize this will change everything. They couldn't help it, too much emotion, and probably too much booze.

Waters touched her cheek gently with his hand. He looked down at her, pulled her mouth to his, they kissed.

They separated and looked at each other. She broke the silence. "Why do you know where she lives?"

They smiled, kissed again, this time, longer and deeper.

CHAPTER 38

"They want a meeting, all of them, at the same time?" Detective Waters asked his partner, again. They were in Waters' car driving to the Spiers' home.

She nodded.

"That's what he said, exactly?"

"That's all I know. He said it'll be information we want."

It was early evening, just after rush hour in the Dallas suburbs. The sun was starting to dive into the clouds to the west. The chief received a call from Ron Spiers' lawyer. He said they wanted to meet with the detectives, and only the detectives, tonight at the Spiers home to talk about the case. They had some information that might be helpful.

"Murph's still tailing Spiers, right?" McBayne asked.

"Yes. He followed him home after work. They're starting to cut back his hours. We probably only have him for a couple more days."

"If he tries anything here, with all these people and everyone at the station knowing where we are, he's got more balls than anyone I know," McBayne said, thinking out loud and trying to figure out what Spiers could be up to.

They completed the trek west in silence. Waters pulled into the driveway. There were two Audis, a Chrysler, and a BMW parked in front of the garage doors. They parked beside the BMW and made their way to the front steps. The detectives proceeded slowly, peering in the front windows and glass door as they approached. They could see people assembled in the living room.

Waters rang the doorbell. A woman wearing a housekeeper's uniform answered. "You must be the detectives. Right this way." She led them through the front door. As they crossed the entrance, they looked upstairs into the sitting room where all the action happened.

They entered the hallway which opened into the sprawling living room.

The housekeeper announced their arrival. "Mr. Spiers, Detectives Waters and McBayne."

"Thank you, Jennifer," Emma Spiers said.

Jennifer left the room.

Standing directly in front of them was Ron Spiers. Emma was a step behind him and to the left. In a semi-circle behind the Spiers was Dr. Charles and Charlene Browning. Jacob and Victoria Daniels were to their left. Behind Spiers and to the right was Jayne Thomas, and beside her to the far right was Shaun and Sky Williams.

Waters quickly scanned the room. All the couples, except the Spiers, looked uncomfortable like they didn't want to be there. He saw his partner focusing on Emma Spiers. Emma kept her eyes straight ahead. Jayne Thomas just looked exhausted; if she suspected Spiers of anything, it wasn't showing.

Spiers skipped the pleasantries and got right to the point. "Detectives, we want to know why this case isn't closed and you continue to harass these people."

Ron was a master of intimidating eye contact and the death stare. It probably made him a great negotiator in business, would make him an even better lawyer if he decided to go that route. Most people would confess to anything after a few minutes of that look.

He didn't give them time to answer. "Look around, Detectives. These people, we're the elite, we're the best at what we do. We make more money in a day than you two make in a month. We're the ones who pay your salaries, not those crackheads and five dollar whores you spend most of your time chasing."

Ron paused. "So, you've discovered our little game. That's fine, good work. But it's no one's business but ours. Do you understand that?"

He waited for an answer. Waters remained silent, they've been trained to let suspects talk as much as they want, they usually get themselves in trouble eventually.

"I realize you'd be jailhouse heroes taking down some rich assholes in Southlake, but it's not going to happen. Nothing devious happened here and you're not going to find anything.

"This woman's husband is dead." He made a motion to Jayne Thomas. "That's a tragedy and an unfortunate accident, but that's all it is. And you dragging this out is making it worse than it has to be. Now, I want this investigation closed, and I want it closed now. Do you understand me, Detectives?"

Waters wasn't sure how to answer. He paused, thinking, but before he could reply, McBayne spoke out. "Mr. Spiers, there's still a lot of inconsistencies in your stories that we're trying to reconcile. And since you won't answer any of our questions, we have to interrogate everyone else and try to piece it together. You were the only one with Frank when he had the accident, right?" She finished the sentence with an accusatory tone.

Waters watched Spiers closely. He gave Detective McBayne a chilling stare, then spoke slowly and deliberately. "Inconsistencies, Detective McBayne? Inconsistencies?"

She gave him a half-smile, then said, "Yes, inconsistencies." She said it slowly like she wasn't sure if he understood the word. "You lied to the police, you're lucky you're not in jail right now like a common criminal."

Detective Waters watched his partner. What was her angle? Was she trying to intimidate Ron Spiers? Not a good person to provoke. He could see the anger start to well up in Spiers' face.

Ron nodded, turned his head, then focused back on Detective McBayne. "You know, I've done some looking into your background. You were a cop for what, just over a year?"

She nodded.

"One year and you got promoted to detective. Is that right?"

She nodded again.

"So, that means deserving men, men who have put in their time, put their lives on the line, have been passed over for promotions because of you? Because you're a woman—you have tits and a cunt. And that's the only reason you're standing here now with that detective shield. You didn't earn it, it was given to you. You can act tough behind that gun and badge, but we all know underneath it there's just a scared little girl who's in way over her head."

Then Spiers turned to him. "I couldn't find out anything about you, Detective Waters. Except you're too chicken shit to carry a gun. It seems you're a sad little man who's going through this world completely unnoticed." He paused.

"I don't know what you're trying to prove with this case. Maybe it's jealousy, maybe you're trying to get back at the popular kids because they were mean to you in school. But I'm warning you, keep pushing this and your pathetic life will get a lot worse."

"You have no idea what I can do. When I'm done, you won't be able to get a job as a security guard at the Walmart in whatever shithole Louisiana town you come from."

He felt his partner watching him, undoubtedly waiting for him to say something. She took a step forward and pointed at Spiers. "Hey, asshole, don't talk to—"

Waters put his arm out in front of her and stepped forward. "Detective, that's okay." He lowered his head and looked down at the floor—rubbed his thumb and index finger against his chin, then looked up and stared directly into Spiers' eyes. "Okay, Mr. Spiers, your concerns are noted. I do have one question." He paused. Spiers and everyone in the room was waiting.

"What happened to the drinks?"

Spiers thought for second. "What drinks?"

"In your statement the night of the accident, you said you went to refresh the drinks for yourself and Mr. Thomas. You heard the crash on your way back. So, what happened to the drink glasses?"

Spiers' eyes darted from side to side. He looked flustered, finally, he answered. "Well, I put them down somewhere. My friend just fell. I was going to his aid, I—"

Waters cut him off. "No, I took pictures of everything, even the sink. No glasses. None on the balcony or the stairs. None in the living room or the kitchen. Nowhere."

He stared at Spiers, arrogantly waiting for a better answer. He didn't get one.

"You know what? Fuck this. Get the hell out of my house. You want to talk to me again, you can go through my lawyers," Spiers said and waved them out.

Waters took a step closer to him, still looking him in the eyes. He said in a low, confident voice. "Ron, I'm going to break my dick off in your ass."

There were a few low gasps from the people gathered around them. Shaun Williams let out a nervous laugh and Charles Browning said, "What did he say?"

"Let's go, Detective," Waters said to his partner without taking his eyes off Spiers. He turned and started walking out of the room. McBayne, looking like she couldn't believe what she just saw, gathered herself and followed him out.

As they descended the front stairs of the house, he sensed Carlie watching him. He turned toward her. "What?"

"Nothing. I'm just glad you didn't say dildo."

They both smiled as they got into their car and drove away.

CHAPTER 39

It was almost quitting time on Friday. Two days had passed since the meeting with Spiers and all the couples, and three weeks since Frank Thomas died. It was just a matter of hours, maybe minutes before the chief gave the word to drop the case. If trying to provoke Ron Spiers didn't work, chances of getting him on anything were fading fast.

The detectives sat at their cubes, trying to work on other cases and complete overdue paperwork. An officer walked a down and out looking suspect by their cubes to the interrogation room, the unmistakable smell of marijuana filled the area as they passed by.

"Anything on the Andrews murder?" Detective McBayne asked her partner.

He looked at her and shook his head, positive she already knew the answer.

Detective Waters clicked his mouse highlighting the Thomas folder icon on his computers desktop in his open cases section. He started to drag it to the "Closed" folder, then stopped. He tapped his mouse against his desk, then clicked the folder again. He shook his head and prepared to complete the action.

His partner's phone rang, she answered it. "Detective McBayne...Emma, hello. How are you?"

He looked over the cube wall, watching her face for any hints of what the discussion was about.

"Is there any chance you can come into the station?... No. Oh, he is, okay... We'll be there in about forty-five minutes... All right, see you then."

She hung up. "That was Emma Spiers. She wants to talk."

"Really. And Ron?"

"No game tonight. She just dropped him off at the airport. He's going to Los Angeles on business."

The detectives gathered their things and headed out of the station.

"How did she sound?" Waters asked as he made the turns towards the outer belt, driving faster than Chance Waters usually does.

"Upset."

McBayne called Murphy to check on the tail of Spiers and reported to Waters. "Murph said he saw Spiers get on the plane, so we're good."

They made the trip to the Spiers' house in relative silence, both pondering what Emma could want to speak to them about. The roads outside of the city were clear, but it was more dark and desolate than normal this evening, they made good time. Detective McBayne had her window rolled halfway down, the breeze blew her hair around.

They pulled into the Spiers' driveway. "Look," Waters said as they approached the house. He motioned to the balcony. Emma Spiers was standing out there by herself, the light shimmering through the doors behind her.

"What's she doing?" he asked.

McBayne released her seatbelt before the car stopped and the warning alarm went off. "Just standing there, I think."

"I hope she's all right," McBayne said. "No idea what to expect with these people, this could be a blessing or a nightmare."

Waters parked the car and the detectives made the now familiar trek up to the house. As they approached the steps, Waters motioned to the front door, it was open slightly. McBayne put her hand on her gun and peeked in, all the lights were off except one upstairs.

"Mrs. Spiers, it's Detectives McBayne and Waters," she said.

"Upstairs," they heard her reply, her voice echoing down the corridors of the large, empty house.

They walked in and looked around, then continued to the stairs. The light from the second floor lit up the stairway. They went upstairs and entered the sitting room. The balcony doors were open, they could see Emma standing outside. They walked through the sitting room, by the ottoman, and onto the balcony.

Emma was alone, looking down at the spot where Frank died. She had been crying but looked more tired than anything.

"We were going to be together," she said, without looking up from the spot on the floor. "He was going to leave Jayne. Ron promised if I helped convince everyone to play, he would let me go.

But he wasn't going to. Deep down, I knew he wouldn't."

She looked at the detectives. "We weren't having an affair. I would have given myself to him. I tried to, but he wouldn't. Not while he was married. That's why he played the game, so we could be together. And to beat Ron at something, anything.

"You know, I tried to leave Ron six years ago. When he found out, he drugged me and paid two bikers to rape me while he videotaped it. He said if I ever talked about leaving him again he would send it to everyone we knew and post it on revenge websites."

She paused, then looked at the detectives. "My family had nothing. We were dirt poor. I just wanted to live the good life, if only for a little while. Just see that side of life for once. That's all I wanted." She looked at Detective McBayne. "Don't ever trade love for money, it's not worth it."

Emma looked back down at the balcony floor. There was still a shadow of blood left outlining the spot where Frank died. "I'm the one who killed Frank. When I went out on the balcony that night, Frank and Ron were arguing. Frank was defending me, making Ron live up to his promise. I knew it wouldn't matter. Nothing Frank could say or do would change Ron. Especially while Frank was beating him at his own game."

She paused. "The wine table was sitting there." She pointed to a spot against the wall by the first balcony door. "I picked it up by the legs, walked up behind Ron and swung it at his head. I wanted to kill him. Ron had Frank by the shirt and saw it coming. He ducked out of the way and pulled Frank in front of him. It hit Frank." She looked at the spot again and began to cry.

She quickly composed herself. "I don't care what happens to me. I just want Ron to pay for this. He made all of us cover it up. He threatened them and had me raped. You should look into his business dealings too. I'll testify, and you can call the rest of them as witnesses."

A man's voice from the end of the balcony interrupted Emma's confession. "Hello, Detectives." It was Ron Spiers, and he was holding a gun. "Oh, your officer was in the line at Starbucks when I passed him in the terminal. He needs to focus on his job more. That's why you people are public servants."

Ron slowly walked over to them. McBayne and Waters didn't move. They were trying to assess the situation.

He looked at Emma. "You want me to go to jail? My own wife. After all I've given you."

McBayne slowly reached down to her side to take out her gun. Ron saw her and pointed his gun at her. "Don't, Detective. I'll shoot you where you stand."

"You don't want to do this," Waters said.

McBayne slowly moved next to Emma.

"Oh, I don't. You think I want to go to prison? I don't think so. It might be time to grow a beard and move to Costa Rica."

"You won't get away with this," Waters said.

"Really, Detective? You don't think I have the resources to disappear forever?" He lifted his gun and pointed it at the two women.

"Detective, I've seen that look before. Shoot him now," Waters told his partner.

"Oh, that's right, Detective Waters. No gun. How are you going to protect your woman?"

"He won't shoot his wife," McBayne said, slowly reaching for her gun.

"Emma, say hi to Frank," Ron said and pointed the gun directly at her.

Carlie quickly moved in front of her. "Don't", she said.

Too late, Spiers pulled the trigger. There was a loud pop, the bullet hit McBayne in the stomach. She fell to the ground in front of Emma.

Waters watched his partner collapse. He took two quick steps and dove at Spiers. As he made contact, Spiers pulled the trigger. The bullet hit Emma in the chest. She fell to the ground beside McBayne, blood spurting out of the hole.

Spiers' gun went flying across the balcony as Waters slammed into him. Spiers grabbed him by the shirt collar and pulled him to the side. Ron got to his feet and held Waters up. He had him firmly by the shirt with one hand and was punching him in the face and chest with the other. Ron had a considerable size and strength advantage over the detective.

Waters blocked the shots and tried to return the blows. He knew he had to get a debilitating shot in quickly.

Spiers started taunting him as he hit the Detective. "What were you going to do to me, Detective? Come on, tell me again." He continued hammering him in the face. Waters turned his head to avoid the full force of the blows. He was desperately trying to avoid a direct shot and getting knocked unconscious.

Waters reached back and got in a solid shot, hitting Spiers in the nose. Blood immediately trickled down to Ron's mouth. He wiped the blood from his nose with the back of his hand, a look of surprise came over him like he was amazed the detective injured him. He smiled, the blood flowing into his mouth and between his teeth, he looked evil and became more motivated by the taste of his own blood.

Spiers grabbed Waters with both hands and threw him against the balcony wall making a solid thud, it almost knocked the detective out. His eyes became blurry and he almost lost consciousness. He shook his head, trying to regain his senses. Spiers grabbed him again, lifting him up to his feet. Waters tried to pull away, but he couldn't break his grip. He reached back and got another shot in at Spiers' jaw.

Spiers smiled. "You're tougher than you look, detective." Then he released him and got into a boxing stance, putting his fists up, his eyes peering over them. "Come on, Detective. Take a shot."

Waters tried to punch him in the face, but Spiers blocked it with his forearm. He tried again, throwing a series of punches. Again, they hit against Spiers' muscular arms. Ron definitely had some boxing training, he knew how to block punches and hit with force. He was also battling a man who would be two or three weight classes below him.

Ron backed up against the balcony rail, continuing to chide Waters, knowing he couldn't hurt him. Waters was getting tired. His face was swollen and bleeding, his vision was getting blurry. He prepared to punch Ron again. He looked over at Carlie on the floor, she wasn't moving, he began to panic. He reached back to hit Spiers again with everything he had. At the last moment, he noticed Spiers hands were up, protecting his face. He let another punch fly, at the last second Waters changed the trajectory of the blow and hit him in the stomach, right in the solar plexus.

The punch landed perfectly. Waters could hear the air rush out of Spiers' chest. Ron doubled over, temporarily paralyzed. Surprised, the detective backed up and looked at the helpless man bent over in front of him. Waters ran into him with as much force as he could summon. Spiers flew back against the balcony rail. Waters ran over to him, grabbed his legs, and with one desperate heave, lifted him over the rail.

Spiers flew backwards the two stories and landed on his head on the driveway. His neck snapped with a gruesome sounding crack. His body twitched as a pool of blood immediately formed around his head.

Waters turned to the two women lying on the balcony behind him. He ran over to Detective McBayne and knelt beside her. He put one hand under her neck and turned her head so she could look at him. He put his other hand on her cheek.

"Carlie."

A horrible feeling overcame him. She wasn't responding. He couldn't breathe, he was losing her forever.

"Carlie," he said again.

She slowly opened her eyes like she just woke out of a deep sleep. She looked around, then focused on him. "You got him?" she said, struggling to speak.

He nodded.

"Chance." She looked up and smiled. "I told you I wasn't going to make it to thirty." Her eyes closed and her head went limp.

"Carlie," he said, his voice cracking. "Please don't die. Please don't die."

CHAPTER 40

The dramatic deaths of beautiful rich people over a high-stakes sex game and the shooting of a detective hit the press hard. Every day more information seemed to come out about the case and the people involved. It became one of those stories people couldn't get enough of, it was a ratings bonanza—everyone had to report on it. In the Dallas-Ft. Worth area, the stories continued for months.

Talk of the "Five for Five" sex game continued long after the criminal part of the case died down. Every talk show did segments on the game. News programs produced multiple stories about it and profiles of the players. They added editorials with their unique political slant on why it happened and what the ramifications were.

Late night comedians cracked jokes about the game and the players. Of course, the family and religious groups got involved and added it to the list of things that were destroying the moral fabric of society.

Social media exploded. Web sites, message boards and smartphone apps based on the game sprung up seemingly overnight. "Five for Five" swingers clubs became popular, even staging tournaments.

Celebrities randomly tweeted numbers in minute and second format to their followers, bragging about their stamina playing the game with their wives and girlfriends. Most of the time they padded their times by many seconds, even minutes.

Charles Browning's medical practice increased exponentially when he was named as one of the players. He had to hire more staff for the new patients he received. Wealthy Asian businessmen traveled thousands of miles seeking him out; believing having Dr. Browning work on them would give them more sexual virility.

Charlene Browning became a real model, landing a popular spread in *Maxim* magazine. In the interview, she gave pointers on how to play the Five for Five game, how men can last longer, and what women should do to get their man off faster.

At first, Shaun Williams tried to hide away in the executive offices of his Audi dealership, but requests to meet him drew him out. In the beginning he wasn't comfortable with the notoriety, but he quickly got used to it. Customers started demanding to meet him before buying a car. They even had incentives like lunch with Shaun for the purchase of a top of the line Audi.

Sky Williams reveled in the attention from the beginning. She did interviews with anyone who would listen. Every appearance ended in some kind of a political statement of how she was trying to help the underprivileged and under served by playing the game.

Jacob Daniels was made a full partner at Taylor Financial, taking Ron Spiers' old position. He and Victoria bought the Spiers' house and moved in as is, furniture and all, including the wine table that was discovered to be the murder weapon. They continued to entertain and treat the balcony and sitting room like a tourist attraction.

Jayne Thomas moved back home with her parents and kept to herself. She never discussed the incident with anyone. Every once in a while a reporter would show up in town, run into her, and try to get her to do an exclusive. Sometimes offering a lot of money, but she wasn't interested.

Detective Waters became the biggest celebrity of them all. He was dubbed by the press as the new Sherlock Holmes, the brilliant super sleuth who used high-tech tools and data to solve murder mysteries. The battle with Spiers on the balcony started to sound like David vs. Goliath. Reporters followed him around morning until night trying to get a statement or find out personal information about the detective. He never once talked to them and that just made them even more persistent.

Waters finally had to move out of his apartment and into a hotel to avoid the press. Eventually, he took an open-ended leave of absence to get away from the limelight.

Before he left, Waters discovered that Spiers was running a Ponzi scheme out of his company. It was about to collapse around him. Spiers had a relationship with a local biker gang. He financed their drug trade, taking a large part of the profits, and used the bikers as his muscle.

Howard Andrews, the accountant at Taylor Financial, was about to discover what Spiers was up to. Spiers had one of the bikers and his girlfriend, aka Shelly, kill Andrews. They were both arrested but got a reduced sentence for confessing they did it, and confirming Spiers part in the murder.

Ron and Emma Spiers were buried side by side in an exclusive Ft. Worth cemetery.

Police Chief O'Halloran got funding to hire more officers and to replace Detectives Waters and McBayne. They even gave him money to put in his tranny bathroom.

CHAPTER 41

Chance Waters was driving westward through the desert on a New Mexico highway. There was one other car far behind him. Waters noticed the headlights turn on as evening approached. He was in the front seat by himself. A shiny metal cylinder rested on the seat beside him.

The sun had just set ahead of him but it was still fairly bright out. The horizon was a stunning combination of orange and red. It might be the most beautiful sunset he'd ever seen, at least, he couldn't remember a better one. The cactus and mountains in the distance made a glorious background against the brilliant colors of the horizon. He had the windows rolled down and the air was as clean and fresh as he could remember.

He turned on the radio. The song "I Can Still Make Cheyenne" by George Strait was playing. He smiled, George was his Dad's favorite singer. He listened to the song's lyrics about a rodeo cowboy who didn't make the short go and his woman kicked him out. He said in a low voice to himself, "Holy shit, you were right. That is sad."

He reached for the radio, pressed a couple buttons, then stopped. He knew this song, 'Peaceful Easy Feeling' by the Eagles. He sang along to the lyrics—his eyes starting to glaze over.

He reached over and turned the volume down, looked up into the rearview mirror, and said in a louder voice. "All right, I'll give you this, that's a good song."

In the mirror a woman's brown hair appeared. It was more messy and curly than normal. Those big blue eyes, the beautiful girl next door face, the person who had made every day since they met a million times better. The girl who scared him worse than he could have imagined when he thought he lost her. They were as different as night and day—two oddly shaped puzzle pieces that fit perfectly together.

Carlie was lying down in the back resting. She had a homemade quilt over her that had white blocks with Eagles song titles and quotes, and colored squares with pictures of the band members at different concerts.

"Good enough to be a rodeo song?" she said and grimaced as she struggled to sit up. She leaned against the back of the passenger seat, letting her arms hang over the front.

"Maybe not that good," he answered.

She reached down and picked up the metal cylinder. "Refill?"

"Sure."

She screwed off the top of the thermos. Waters held up his coffee cup without looking and she filled it. He took a drink. "I really do make good coffee."

She nodded.

"How are you feeling?"

"Better. Still a little sore. Now it feels like when I had my appendix out."

"Drink your cranberry juice. It helps fight infections."

She took a sip from a straw coming out of a plastic bottle. "Okay, but we'll have to stop so I can pee again."

"That's fine, we're in no hurry." He looked at her in the mirror. "Hey, it's almost dusk. Want me to pull over so you can take your clothes off and crawl around in the desert?"

She smiled. "Detective Waters, six months ago you wouldn't even swear around me. Now you're talking like a pervert."

"What if there's a snake with a beaver head out there who needs to tell you something?"

"I barely made it to twenty-eight. Still have two more years till thirty, smart guy. And it was a muskrat head."

"Oh right, sorry."

They looked at each other in the mirror. She put her hand on his shoulder. He placed his on top of hers and gave it a squeeze. He reached down and turned up the radio. They started singing her favorite Eagles song together.

On the side of the road they passed a sign that said, "Winslow, AZ - 128 miles."

END

ABOUT THE AUTHOR

When Jeremy Lawrence won his first writing award in High School, it wasn't thanks to a glowing submission (he didn't enter one). So, he headed off to college with a poetry scholarship, but his real aspiration was a baseball career.

He soon discovered he had a unique talent for programming computers, and so the baseball and writing would have to wait. Fast-forward twenty-five years, Lawrence is now the proud author of thousands of computer programs with his literary output limited to greeting cards and Facebook essays.

In the end it was a family tragedy that convinced Lawrence life was too short to pass with his stories still inside him, and so he wrote his debut novel, Already Gone, a comedic murder mystery simmering with intrigue, and a dash of romance.

A lifelong Eagles fan, Lawrence is currently working on the second book in the three book series, all inspired by some of his favorite songs (and yes, that is a band shirt in his headshot). When he isn't writing he can be found coaching girls' softball, boating and kayaking the pristine waters of the Florida Keys, and being a proud father to his two gorgeous daughters.

Made in the USA
Las Vegas, NV
12 September 2021